I0531607

Celebration of Life

Book One of the Celebration Trilogy

Patricia Gauthier

8/9/2012

bstract of the document here. The abstract is typically a short summary of the contents of the document.]

Chapter 1

Trish Haywood felt inadequate having to admit to anyone that she didn't understand why people needed romance. After all, she did run a company that organized romantic weddings every day. She knew how to plan it but she didn't pretend to understand it. "I don't know anything about romance. To me the movie Titanic just doesn't make any sense. Why would a woman hold onto a necklace for eighty years just to throw it into the sea? It wasn't even Jack's necklace to begin with. What was the sea going to do with it anyway? I would have cashed it in long before that." Trish argued yet again to her friend Candy.

"Oh you just don't understand how important the necklace was to Rose." Candy said exasperated as she raised her hands in surrender.

"But Jack didn't give her the necklace!" Trish said. "You can try to explain it to me again, like the one million other times you've tried, but it'll never make sense."

"Love doesn't always make sense now does it?"

"I guess I wouldn't know about that since I've never been in love." Trish reminded her. "But if throwing an expensive necklace overboard is love you can just count me out . I'm too practical to go ga ga over a man I barley know. You do realize she's only known Jack for about forty eight hours, right? Plus, if it means that much to Rose why did she wait sixty five years to throw it back to Jack? And another thing........."

"Stop! I get it. It's not logical. Is everything in life logical? We're talking about emotions here and I know you have them, whether you want to admit it or not. Boy, those nuns really did a number on you didn't they."

Candy was tired of having the same old conversation with Trish and decided to change the subject. "So how's the party planning business going lately?" Candy asked.

"Oh. It's going great so far. I've just started a charity of my own actually. It's a program I designed to have children go on supervised horseback rides to help raise funds for school projects. I donate the pizza, pop and cookies and the school sets their own price to charge for the rides. I rotate different schools each month. It's a lot of fun. Melissa's doing it with me."

"Figures you'd do something for kids. I've never seen anyone enjoy other people's children as much as you. Why do you think that is?"

"Easy. I know eventually they're going home. It's the best of both worlds. Play a little and then send them on their way."

"I think you need one of your own." Candy said.

"Ha, ha. You know I can't even keep a house plant alive, let alone a human being. Besides, I'm too selfish to share my life with anyone. I like not having to ask anyone else's opinion when I'm making a decision. I'll just get a cat or something if I get lonely, which I'm not." Trish looked at her watch and jumped up. "I'm going to be late. Catch ya ' later." She flew out of the restaurant at a brisk walk.

Whew. Dodged a bullet on that one. Trish knew the next thing coming out of Candy's mouth was how she knew the perfect guy for Trish. She knew the drill by heart. He was blah, blah, blah, and he had blah, blah, blah. No, thank you very much. If he's so great why didn't she just keep him for herself? Besides, her business took up all of her weekends and men didn't understand that Celebrations was everything to her. Party planning was more work than most people realized, especially for the bridezillas of the world. Charity functions were very rewarding to plan but you had to offer the right bait and, frankly, she had her doubts about the bachelor/bachelorette auction she had planned for tomorrow night. Again, not having a romantic bone in her body, she didn't understand the draw to such functions. It made her feel like she was in the human trafficking business. They certainly hadn't had any trouble getting a group of singles to volunteer for the event. It wasn't something Trish would ever consider doing herself. *I guess if you were desperate.* Oh well, not her problem. You got to give the customer what they want.

The auction went better than expected for her and the charity that held it, making more money tonight than they ever had before. In fact it shattered all previous events to bits. Thank goodness the night was almost over, she was bushed. She tossed the bachelor/bachelorette catalog on the desk of the small office Trish had been using for the night. Someone knocked on the door jam and, without looking up, Trish told them to come in.

"Hi. May I help you?" Staring back at her was the most beautiful and strikingly handsome man she had ever seen. No scratch that, he looked like a Greek god. About six four with thick, dark walnut colored, wavy hair that laid on top of his shirt collar. His broad muscular shoulders drew the eye down to a narrow waist without an ounce of fat on it. He had piercing blue eyes, darker than Trish's even, with a strong, straight nose and full, firm lips. Adonis sprang to mind.

"I arrived late and missed the auction. I was wondering if you could help me make a selection from the catalog by telling me who was still available."

His voice was deep, disc jockey deep, and it made Trish's insides vibrate when he spoke.

"Sure. Why don't you tell me what type of date you're interested in and I'll look it up for you Mr.---?" Trish wanted to make sure he was even interested in a woman, he could be gay after all. She didn't want to offend anyone.

"Sinclair. Davis Sinclair. And you are?"

"Trish Haywood." They shook hands and the electricity that zapped Trish almost made her jump. "Nice to meet you, Mr. Sinclair."

Davis looked through the catalog and a puzzled look came to his face. "I 'm looking for someone specific, but I can't find her picture in here."

"Oh. Do you know her name? Maybe I can look it up on the computer for you." Well that answered the gay question, Trish thought.

"Yes. Her name is Trish Haywood." Trish looked up to his smiling face. Oh god. He has dimples too! Long, thin dimples that caressed his sensuous mouth. Trish was a sucker for dimples.

"Ah. Well, I'm not part of the auction. I'm just the organizer. Maybe there's someone else you're interested in.?"

"But you are single, right?" Davis stared down at her with his deep blue eyes. She had to look away to break the spell they put her under.

"Doesn't matter. I'm not for sale. Besides, I'm married to my business, and I have a no dating policy that I strictly adhere to."

"We'll see. I'm very persistent when I want something bad enough. I think you'd be worth any effort I put into it." And with that he turned around and walked out the door.

What a hunk. Too bad. Dating was not on Trish's favorite things to do list. After a couple of heartbreaking relationships she came to the realization that there are other things in life to enjoy. She had never been loved by anyone, ever. Her childhood had been cold and uncaring, being taken care of by the nuns out of obligation. No one ever held her, comforted her when she was sick, lovingly tended to her cuts and scrapes. When she was twenty one and turned out of the convent, no one walked her to the door or even cared if she was there or not, no one was going to be sorry to see her go. No one wished her well. Trish had come to the conclusion long ago that she was unlovable and that was how she still viewed herself today. Some people were meant to stay single and she considered herself one of them. Things in the love department had never worked out for Trish. She tried dating all different types of men. Nerds, professionals, she even dated a doorman once. She tried the smother them tactic and the hands-off approach and everything in between tactic, nothing worked for her so she decided she wouldn't waste anymore evenings suffering with some guy when there were so many other things to do. Trish was never one to mind being alone. If she wanted to go to the show or out to dinner she did it by herself. She didn't need anyone to keep her company. If she had learned anything from her childhood, it was how to be alone. She was flying solo and that was just fine with her.

"Trish we've got a problem." Mrs. Sullivan said as she breezed into the office. "My nephew is new in town and was late arriving. I'm very sorry, but we need to arrange a bachelorette for him. He's quite well off and I'm sure he'd be very generous in his donation."

"No problem. Let's look through the catalog and see who's still available." Trish needed to handle this delicately since Mrs. Sullivan was chairman of the fund raising committee.

"Well, he has a specific person in mind." Trish started to get a sinking feeling in the pit of her stomach. Dread invaded her.

"Okay, who did he have in mind?"

"You." Mrs. Sullivan said with a stern look on her face. Being the chairperson of the fundraising committee gave her more clout when it came to demands than the average person and Trish wanted the repeat business. She might just have to cave on this one. She gave it one last shot.

"Mrs. Sullivan I've already met your nephew and explained to him that I'm not available. If there's someone else he could select I'll do whatever necessary to accommodate him, but the answer is still no."

"As I've said he's very generous. He has offered to match whatever donations we've received tonight if this can be arranged. Do I need to tell you how important it is to the Children With A Wish Foundation to double our already record breaking funds. Not to mention how grateful I personally would be."

Crap. "All right Mrs. Sullivan. You win. Have Mr. Sinclair call my office to make the arrangements with my assistant."

"Oh thank you Trish. I promise you won't regret it and I owe you one."

Yeah. You owe me more than one she thought. I guess I'll live through it but I won't like it. Let's face it, I already regret it. Too bad he needs his auntie to arrange his dates for him. He probably has the personality of a toad. With a sigh Trish left the convention center. Now all she wanted was a cup of tea and a good book. If she was lucky maybe there'd be a good old movie on television tonight. Trish liked the background noise of the television even when she was reading her books. Most nights she slept on the couch instead of the bed. Beds were just too big and empty and cold. Sleeping on the couch made her feel safe and secure, she liked that snuggled in feeling the couch gave her. Like someone had their arms around you but you could still move around. With all that going on there wouldn't be time to think about Davis Sinclair.

When she walked into her office the next day her assistant, Melissa was already at her desk. God what a gem she was. Good with customers, prompt and efficient. Trish didn't know what she would do without her. True, she paid her well, but it certainly wasn't enough for the peace of mind she gave Trish. Because of this she always tried to surprise her with unexpected gifts, today she would give her a small flower arrangement for her desk.

"Wow. Thanks! I guess everything went well last night then. Did you guys reach your donation goal?"

"Reached it, passed up the old record, and doubled it. Although, it was at great personal sacrifice to me. There will be a Mr. Davis Sinclair calling to set up a date with me. See what

5

evening you can fit him in and if Mrs. Sullivan calls, just so you know, she owes me big time."

"Wait. Let me get this straight. You are going out on a date?"

"Yep. I sold my soul to the devil in order to double the donations." As she turned and walked into her office Melissa was right on her heels. When Trish turned around she ran right into her. Melissa's eyes were bulging and her mouth was gaping open. Total shock.

"You don't' date. Ever. Never since I've been here. Come on. Out with it and don't skip any of the little details." Melissa said and proceeded to sit down with her full and undivided attention on Trish. All she needed was some popcorn and a diet soda to complete the show.

Trish explained the whole ugly story to Melissa. She did kind of leave out the Adonis body and fantastic eyes and the dimples but other than that she managed to get the story out.

"Holy hell. Sounds like this guy's got it bad for you."

"This guy doesn't even know me. Now how about we get a little work done around here." Melissa left the room . Thank goodness. Now Trish could get back to business as usual.

Chapter 2

It didn't take long for Davis Sinclair to call, or rather his secretary. He had a formal dinner to attend this Thursday night and wanted to know if Trish could accompany him. Melissa put the call on hold and knocked on Trish's door.

"Mr. Sinclair's secretary is on the phone. He wants you to go to a formal dinner with him this Thursday night at 7:00 p.m. Is that okay?"

"Yeah. I may as well get it over with."

"That's the spirit!" Melissa said.

Figures it would be a formal affair. He just seemed to be the formal type. Although Trish knew you shouldn't judge a book by its cover she was in no mood to be kind. *I guess I'll just have to put on my big girl panties and deal with it* she thought. Shit, she hated this whole situation and resented being put into it.

When Thursday arrived Trish tried not to think of the impending doom of dating. In reality it didn't really matter if it went well or not she reasoned. They'd never see each other again anyway. No sweat. I can do this with a blindfold on, she thought. Pep talk over.

Later in the day Melissa told her that Davis was running late and would she mind taking a cab to the banquet hall and meeting him there instead of him picking her up. *Okay by me.*

Trish took a long, hot bath and then carefully applied her make-up. Because it was formal and evening she was a bit heavier with the eye shadow and mascara than she would normally be. If you're going to do something you may as well do it right. She selected a long blue gown that gradually shaded from light blue on the bodice to a midnight blue at the bottom and every different shade of blue in between. It reminded Trish of a melting candle the way the colors ran together in a molten, flowing way. The entire gown had a slight shimmer to it because of the silver threads that ran the entire length of the gown. Spaghetti straps criss-crossed at the low cut halter back. The gown clung to each and every curve God had given her, and

7

showed just the slightest cleavage at the scooped neckline. Its lines were simple, straight and elegant. The long, slim skirt hugged her in all the right places and had a slit up the side that went to her mid-thigh. Very sexy. Trish wore her hair up in a twist and secured it with a rhinestone and sapphire comb that she secured into the twist. Simple diamond stud earrings adorned her ears. A Silver clutch style bag and dyed-to-match high heeled shoes finished the look. As she examined herself in the mirror she was pleased. The blue of the dress complimented the color of her deep blue eyes and her dark auburn hair. Wearing her hair up gave the illusion of a longer neck and a long, sleek silhouette. With a deep cleansing breath Trish went out to the waiting cab.

Trish didn't know who taught the cab driver how to drive but she thought they would never get there. Her granny drove faster than this guy, that is if she had one. Frustration only added to her anxiety as she entered the banquet hall. The sooner she got there the sooner she could leave, and that, after all, was the goal.

Davis Sinclair stood with his back to the entrance with a couple of lawyers Trish recognized from the law practice she used. Suddenly two of the men's mouths dropped open in amazement while they watched Trish make her entrance.

"Hi Davis. Am I late? The driver took forever to get here." He laid a quick, gentle kiss on her temple.

"No, no. Not a problem. You look beautiful. Thank you for coming." Davis had to swallow hard before he could continue. "Let me introduce you to a couple of my friends. Larry Harmon and Steve Conner, meet Trish Haywood. Larry and Steve work with me at the law firm."

"Nice to meet you." Trish said and shook both their hands. No zing there but that little kiss Davis had given her put knots in her stomach. God he was sexy. *Down girl.* Davis Sinclair certainly knew how to fill out a tuxedo. Some women went for a man in uniform but Trish was the more formal type. That is if she had a type at all. He smelled musky and earthy at the same time. Heady stuff. Sexy. Sensual. Get a grip, she thought, and did a mental shake-down. As she looked up, auntie dear was approaching. She again plastered on a smile as Mrs. Sullivan approached them, she kept reminding herself to be nice.

"Trish. You remember my aunt, Mrs. Sullivan?" Davis said.

"Yes. Of course. How are you Mrs. Sullivan?" Trish shook her hand.

"Oh don't you two make a lovely couple. Davis I applaud your taste in women. Trish darling you look just stunning. You'll be the envy of all the ladies this evening, and of course all the men as well." She tossed a look at Larry and Steve, who nodded in agreement.

"Thank you." Trish smiled.

"Davis, Larry, and Steve, Mr. Sullivan has asked that you meet him in the conference room down the hall for a moment. Some sort of emergency or something or other. I'll get Trish settled in for you Davis. Come my dear."

Mrs. Sullivan took her straight to an empty banquet table, told her to have a seat, nicely of course, and promptly abandoned her. Trish sat at the round banquet table and took in the sights. You never knew what ideas you could pick-up from someone else. The centerpieces on the tables were tall and elaborate with large blue hydrangeas, purple hyacinths, lily of the valley and fern greens with small peacock feathers to accent the vivid colors of the flowers. The tablecloths in teal blue matched the centerpieces, with green cloth napkins at each place setting. Crystal and gold chandeliers hung from the ceiling and crystal sconces adorned the champagne colored walls dotted with insets of champagne colored flocked wallpaper. It gave a very elegant feel to the room. Rather formal and perfect for this bunch of stuffed shirts, Trish thought to herself. A string quartet was seated in the corner as it serenaded the guests with soft, relaxing classical music. As the guests took their seats Trish's table filled quickly. Everyone was there except Davis. Trish waited for Davis, expecting him to take the empty chair next to her any minute. As Trish looked up toward the outside hallway she saw a waiter wheeling a metal cart filled with covered dishes of food. Suddenly Trish was uneasy. She didn't know anyone here except for Davis and his aunt, and they weren't anywhere in sight. Apparently she was worrying for nothing because everyone was ignoring her completely. No one at her table would even make eye contact with her. Friendly group here, she thought. She didn't even know what the purpose of the banquet was or who put it on. Trish fussed nervously with the purse in her lap, trying to convince herself not to run from the room and go home. The first course was served. Spinach salad. Great. Something to cling to your front tooth when you smiled. Good thing she didn't feel like smiling, far from it. She pretended to eat, wondering where Davis was and why he wasn't at the table. This was getting embarrassing. The main course was salmon with twice whipped potatoes and steamed veggies. Still no Davis. Trish's face flushed red and warm with anger. How rude is this? Invite someone to dinner and then don't see them the rest of the night. She had a cup of coffee after dinner and fidgeted some more with her purse. Someone came to the podium and the speeches began. Trish had no idea what the guy up there was talking about or who. By now she really didn't care. She decided to give him fifteen more minutes and then she was getting out of there.

Time's up. Now Trish was so pissed she was ready to spit tacks. Who did this jackass think he was? As far as she was concerned her obligations had been met. Trish walked to the coat check girl and asked her to call her a cab and give her a piece of note paper so she could leave Davis a scathing note.

Davis:

Thank you for the evening.

Conversation could have been better though.

Maybe you could work on that.

Trish

When the cab arrived she left, fuming. How insulting. How rude. Now she remembered why she didn't do this anymore. Too degrading. Too humiliating. Maybe I will get that cat after all she thought to herself. Deep cleansing breaths she kept telling herself. Calm down. Nothing you can do about it. Mrs. Sullivan had turned out to be just as rude as Davis, must be genetic. It was Mrs. Sullivan's fault Trish had been put in this situation in the first place. Last time I let someone push me into doing something I know is not going to end well.

Davis sat in the conference room and checked his watch yet again, wondering how Trish was getting along at the banquet. Of all the times to have an emergency with a client it had to be the one time he had a knock-out for a date. He let his mind wander to all of Trish's glorious curves that god had put in all the right places. The brief glimpse of her shapely leg through the high cut slit of her dress made his blood pressure soar with desire.

Davis wondered what that thick, beautiful auburn hair of hers would feel like in his hands and while it was running through his fingers. Trish's sapphire blue eyes gazing at him with wanting, while he caressed her creamy smooth skin. He could barely control the urge to shoot out of his seat and find her.

Larry suddenly startled Davis back to reality. Jake Sullivan, his uncle, was apologizing to everyone once again for interrupting their evening.

"Here at the Sullivan Law Firm our clients pay their fees with the expectation of service being available at all hours of the day and night. That's what has built our business from a small private practice to a multi-national corporation and I'm not willing to risk our reputation now. We'll all stay here until this problem is resolved to the client's satisfaction."

Davis loosened his tie with a sigh of resignation. Well, so much for dating Trish Haywood. Davis expected her to be angry, anyone would be in the same situation. Just another thing he would have to deal with later.

When Trish arrived at work the next day Melissa was waiting, and not very patiently either.

"Well. Spill it. All the gory details. Leave nothing out. Go."

"Not much to tell really. I got there. He introduced me to a couple of friends. Mrs. Sullivan came up and told him there was a quick meeting in the conference room so he left. Never saw him again the rest of the night. Ate dinner alone. Listened to a couple of speeches, alone. Finally I called a cab and left, alone. Left him a nasty note that I'm not even sure he got. The end."

"Wait. You're telling me he never said a word to you all night. How long did you wait for him?"

"A couple of hours." Trish answered. "It was the most insulting, humiliating evening of my life and, damn it, I looked fantastic."

"I don't believe it. You have really shitty luck with men."

"Don't I know it, now you understand the no dating policy I should have stuck with. Although I've come to think of it as more of a skill that I'm just now realizing I alone possess. Now let's get to my messages. I think I have a pretty crazy day today."

"Yeah. Half hour until your presentation for Day to Day. I have all the slides loaded into the projector for you already."

11

"Right. I'll be in the conference room setting-up the displays. Make sure the coffee is fresh for them and can you bring in the packets I prepared and lay them out on the conference table. You know the drill."

Trish had put in a lot of time on this presentation. It had the potential to do a lot of repeat business for her company, so it had to be just right. Luckily, Trish never had trouble with public speaking. She actually enjoyed it because she knew her business inside and out.

During the presentation, which was going even better than she had expected, Trish heard some raised voices in the lobby followed by a tentative knock on the door. Frowning Trish asked to be excused and cracked the door open. There she saw an ashen faced Melissa.

"What's up Melissa?" she whispered tersely.

"Sorry to interrupt but Mr. Sinclair is here and he *very strongly* insists on seeing you. Now. Right now."

"Did you tell him I was in a meeting?"

"Yes, but he didn't seem to care." Melissa said apolitically.

"Okay. Tell him I'll be there in a minute. Better yet. Put him in my office and make sure you shut the door." *This guy is dead meat.*

Trish turned to her clients and asked to be excused for a moment. She stopped by Melissa's desk and asked her to serve the pastry and refreshments while she was gone. "Try to get a feel for the mood of the room while you're at it. Let me know if I'll need to do some damage control."

Trish walked into her office, fuming. Before she could speak Davis jumped up and whirled on her. "What the hell is this?" he flung the note she had left him onto her desk.

"I believe it's called a note. You know, a form of communication. Oh wait. Maybe you don't know. Let me explain. Civilized people use it to tell other people things. Simple enough, or do you need further explanation?" Trish said dryly. She crossed her arms over her chest and tapped her high-heeled foot in anger.

"Very funny. I get it." Davis sneered. "I didn't mean to abandon you last night but it just couldn't be helped."

"No. I don't think you do understand, but then it's not my job to teach you either. I have never been treated so badly in my life! I sat at that damn table for two hours waiting for you, or at least a message from you, and I got nothing. I didn't know a soul there.

Your aunt dumped me at our table and left me there, alone. I have never been treated so rudely in my entire life. I thought people like you went to special schools to learn manners. Maybe you flunked, I don't know, but at least your aunt could have checked on me or something. The people at my table wouldn't even make eye contact with me, let alone talk to me."

"Okay, just settle down a minute." Davis said.

"Oh no you don't! You come into my office, and interrupt my meeting you'll damn well listen to what I have to say." By now Trish was in his face yelling and poking her index finger into the same spot on his muscular chest as she punctuated each word with a poke until he flinched.

"I'm sorry O.K.? There was a very important client that was in a very bad situation and we had to take care of it immediately. I should have explained it to you. I'm really sorry."

"You mean like the important client you just interrupted me for? Here's a little news flash for you pal, I have important clients too and damn you for thinking you can interrupt my meeting because you were pissed."

"Ouch. I deserved that too." Davis looked sorry. Looks could be deceiving she told herself. "It's just that I was really looking forward to spending some time with you, and then I got your note. I didn't have your phone number and I realize as I say them out loud they're lame excuses for interrupting your meeting. Sorry again, I was only thinking of myself." Davis hung his head in mock shame.

"Okay. We'll just chalk it up to experience and move on. Are we done here then because I was in the middle of a presentation that I need to get back to." Trish said impatiently.

"One other thing." Davis said holding his hand up. "When can we go out again?"

"Never. Anything else?" Trish said as she headed for the door. Davis reached it before she did and blocked her exit. Angry again, Trish took a deep breath. "You still owe me a date."

"No I don't. I came, I ate and I left. If you weren't there for it that's not my fault. Now get out of my way."

Davis stepped aside and opened the door for her. As she walked through he said "I'll call you." She gave him a sideways glance that would kill any other mortal man and went back to her meeting. Davis heard her "Sorry for the interruption everyone. If you'll take your seats we can resume the meeting." Trish said with a serenity Davis hadn't expected to hear.

Boy she was a cool one Davis thought. Tough nut to crack. So maybe he had been rude to leave her at the banquet like that but it wasn't like he had been given a choice. When the boss barks you listen., he justified. Davis was determined to see Trish again. She was even more beautiful when she was mad, and that thought made him smile as he walked back to his office. What he needed was a plan. A little schmoozing to the assistant and he could have a real ally in her. He'd have to send Melissa some flowers to apologize for the scene he caused in the lobby. Build a friendly relationship with her to get to Trish. Nothing romantic you understand. Just a co-conspirator. Someone to put in a good word or two on his behalf. If he got desperate he could always go to his aunt. He'd have to think about that. Trish was just as mad at Sylvia as she was with Davis, besides, he couldn't hide behind auntie's skirts forever. Suddenly in a much better mood, he began to whistle a happy little tune as he strolled into his office. It's good to have a plan. Phase one is Melissa.

After several weeks of buttering-up Melissa, Davis had a pretty good idea of Trish's schedule and habits. Now was the time for attack. He had to keep it very low key. Of all the times he had seen Trish in Celebrations since the yelling Trish had never even paid him any attention. She completely ignored him and spoke only to Melissa. Trish probably thought he was hitting on Melissa, which was fine with him. At least she had stopped yelling at him and hadn't kicked him out of the office. One thing was for sure, he had learned that strong arming Trish just plain pissed her off. He didn't even understand why it was so important to win her over. He had to be crazy. There were plenty of fish in the sea but she challenged him. Beautiful. Intelligent. Sexy. Stubborn. But mostly he didn't like to lose. Let's see how long she could hold out when he poured on the charm.

Most Tuesday night's Trish went to the movies. There was a sweet little theater a few blocks from her apartment that she could walk to when the weather was nice. They usually ran decent flicks, sometimes even classics. Trish liked the kind of movie that would take her mind off everything for a couple of hours. Nothing deep. Nothing depressing. Entertainment pure and simple. Sometimes a horror flick around Halloween. Tonight was comedy. Trish stopped home and changed into her most comfortable jeans, a t-shirt and a flannel button down that she left unbuttoned and wore like a sweater over that. Tennis shoes and a pair of striped socks finished the outfit. She stopped by the pizzeria and bought a slice and a Mountain Dew while she walked to the theater. Once finished with her dinner, she went up to the ticket window and bought her ticket. Nothing from the snack bar. She exceeded her calorie intake with the pizza. She found herself an aisle seat, as was her habit, and waited for the coming attractions. She had no idea what was coming and if she had would have run from the theater all the way home she thought later.

Davis entered at the other end of the aisle Trish was seated at and strolled to the seat next to her. "Is this seat taken?" he asked as innocently as possible. She looked around to an almost empty theater and wondered why someone had to pick this seat of all the seats available. She didn't like sharing an armrest with anyone, especially a complete stranger. As she looked up she saw him. "Davis. What are you doing here?" Trish struggled to make sense of the situation.

"I came to see a movie. I looked up and saw you here and thought I'd join you." He sat down next to her knowing she wouldn't be rude enough to tell him to scram.

"It's a free country. Do what you want." She said and looked at the screen. *Crap, crap, and triple crap.* How was she supposed to concentrate on the movie with him sitting right next to her? On top of it he smelled great too. Moving her seat wouldn't help, the theater was too empty and he'd just follow her anyway. Sitting next to a stranger would freak them out and Davis would just sit on the other side of her. She was stuck. Trish crossed her arms over her chest, pissed.

"Do you live around here?"

"Yeah. Just a few blocks. How about you? You seem more of the upscale type for this neighborhood."

"A friend of mine suggested this theater for its quiet atmosphere." He said sweetly.

15

Trish was suddenly anxious for the coming attractions to start. He was making her nervous. She came here to relax. Suddenly the lights went down and the show began. *Thank God.*

Casually, Davis put his arm on the back of her seat. He leaned very close to her ear and whispered "I hope you don't mind. This way we don't have to share the armrest." His hot breath sent a shiver down her spine as he spoke in his deep voice. Man he's sexy. She could feel the heat from his body as she sat there pretending to pay attention to the movie. Halfway through the movie she felt him playing with her hair. She turned and looked at him and realized he was staring at her with a smile on his face. "You know your hair is beautiful. It's so soft and silky. Feels just the way I imagined it would. Smells good too."

"Thanks" Trish said as his fingers brushed the back of her neck while stroking her hair. She closed her eyes momentarily and enjoyed the jolts of electricity traveling down her spine. When his hand started massaging her neck she tensed.

"You seem kind of tense. You need to get out and relax more. Here, I'll work the kinks out for you."

The sensations coursing through her body were driving her wild. Did he know what he was doing to her? Did he care that he was sending her into orbit? She turned and looked at him. Oh yeah, he knew alright. Well two could play that game, she thought. She faked a few coughs and cleared her throat as she leaned in very close to his ear and whispered. "Would you mind if I had a sip of your pop? I have a tickle in my throat." She smiled sweetly.

As she leaned in he could see down her scoop necked t-shirt to the cleavage beneath her hot red bra. Her breath was hot and sweet on his ear and she smelled of lavender. Not overly strong. You had to be close to smell it, and thank god he was.

"Sure. No problem." As he handed her the cup she smiled sweetly at him, showing her perfect white teeth.

"Thanks. You saved my life here." He had to close his eyes as she slowly and sensuously took the straw into her mouth. She pulled the straw up a little and then pushed it back into the cup while her lips lingered at the top of the straw. Davis broke into a whole body sweat as she fondled the straw with her hands and mouth sensuously. She caressed his thigh to get his attention and handed him back the cup. He suddenly looked pale and thirsty.

"Are you feeling all right? You look sort of pale." She gave him her most sincere look.

He smiled. "Yeah. I'm great." *Liar*. He knew he was near the edge, sweating, as he replaced the cup into the built in holder. He liked her too much, he thought, as he turned his attention back to the movie. By now he had no idea what the movie was about. Good thing there wasn't going to be a written test about it afterward.

They watched the rest of the movie in silence. As the lights came on in the theater they both stood and stretched. As Trish headed out of the theater Davis took her hand in his. It felt good, so she didn't struggle to pull it away. Everyone needed some small pleasures in life. Once they were out on the sidewalk Davis asked "You're not walking home alone are you?"

"Sure. I do it all the time. It's a pretty safe neighborhood."

"Would you mind if I walked with you? I'd never forgive myself if something happened to you."

"If it means that much to you, you're welcome to join me. But I'm not asking you in."

"Fair enough." Davis took her hand back into his for the rest of the walk home. Neither one talked about the movie because, frankly, they had no idea what they'd just seen. So they walked, contented with the street noises and their small talk until they reached her building.

When they arrived at the steps of her building Davis pulled her into his arms and kissed her very lightly on the lips. Her arms circled his neck as she urged him on with her own tongue, exploring the depths of his strong, firm mouth. Trish buried her hands in his hair and pressed the length of her body against his as he deepened their kisses, loosing track of time and reality as the electric currents ran throughout her entire body, she sizzled with excitement. When they finally broke apart Trish had to catch her breath before she could talk. "Wow. You're really, really good at that." She raised her fingers to her slightly swollen lips.

"You are too. You continue to surprise me." He smiled and gently touched her cheek. "Goodnight. Sleep tight." and he

17

walked away slowly as she watched from the stoop of the apartment building. He looked back once and gave a casual wave. She waved back as he disappeared into the night.

Yeah, like she was going to get any sleep after that make-out session. It was times like this she regretted her no dating rule. She was sure her hormones would settle down in a few days. She'd just have to wait it out. When you play with fire you get burned she reminded herself.

When she got into her apartment she turned on the television and made herself a cup of tea trying to focus on completing her bedtime routine. Shower, shave, read, brush your teeth and fall asleep in front of the television. Same shit, different day. Except tonight she fell asleep with a smile on her slightly swollen, well kissed lips.

Davis was shaken all the way down to his toes. What started out as a fun challenge to him, a game even, turned suddenly into a raging urge to have her. Who was he kidding? He wanted her from the first time he saw her and nothing was going to stop him now. Not after a make-out session like that one. He still felt those kisses on his lips. But he had other considerations besides his hormones so he had to keep his wits about him. He had his Aimee to think about. When his ex-wife, Jasmine, walked out on them, he vowed that his little girl would be his main priority, and he had kept that vow for the last three years. Aimee was the light of his life. At only four years-old she had him wrapped around her little finger and he knew it, but was helpless to do anything about it. Truth be told, he really didn't want to do anything about it. Aimee's nanny, Josie, however, didn't agree. Too bad. My house. My kid. My rules. Now that Aimee was getting a little older he felt it was time to get back into the dating scene again. He went out a few times before they moved from Boston and came to Harbor Springs, but no one special. Before Trish that is. How could he have thought that life in Harbor Springs would be quieter and slower? At first it was quiet. Comfortable. He wanted a small town atmosphere to raise Aimee in. Someplace where you knew who your neighbors were and made lasting friendships. Harbor Springs seemed like just the place. Although his parents were gone, he still had his Aunt Sylvia and Uncle Jake. Really the only family he had, and they treated him and Aimee just like their own son and granddaughter. Aimee adored Aunt Sylvia and Davis was grateful when Uncle Jake took him into the law firm. Even though they never had children of their own, they understood and supported his efforts at raising Aimee in a small town. Being the little girly, girl Aimee was, she needed the attention and support of a loving female in her life. Josie, her nanny, loved his little girl and took very good care of her but it's not the same as family. He wanted to give that to Aimee. A loving family life that he never had. He would just have to wait and see where things went with the lovely Trish Haywood.

For the next few weeks Davis continued to meet Trish at the theater on Tuesday nights. Nothing official, mind you. Just two friends meeting at the show if they could make it. Somehow both of them managed to make it every week. The only change was now they sat in the make-out section instead of in the center of the theater. They became comfortable in each other's company. Occasionally they would stop for coffee at the diner on the corner after the movie, talking for hours and often loosing track of time.

At first Trish was surprised to learn that Davis had a four year-old daughter. Every time he spoke about her his beautiful blue eyes would light up, and the love for her poured out of him. Trish respected him for choosing to move to Harbor Springs for her. It was nice to know he was capable of such love and devotion. Not all men would be that committed to their children, let alone up-root their lives for them.

Davis was the first man that didn't bore her to tears with long, drawn-out stories about their work. Trish didn't have to struggle to sit and listen to Davis. He held her attention, especially when he told funny stories of Aimee's antics. Kids really do say the darndest things. Davis had recently had his helper day at Aimee's pre-school and regaled her with such hilarious stories Trish laughed until she cried. All these stories had Trish even more excited about the new charity she and Melissa were starting for the kids. This Saturday would be their first event and she hoped it went smoothly. She'd keep her fingers crossed.

Chapter 4

Today was the big day. Their first charity event for their very own charity. The horses were saddled and ready to go. Trish and Melissa had the kid's safety helmets ready. Pizza was on its way along with the pop and cookies. As the parents arrived with their children each group was given safety instructions. The kids were scared and excited at the same time. Trish decided to use the outdoor arena since it was a beautiful fall day. Unseasonably warm with bright sunshine. Parents helped pass out the pizza and pop, saving the cookies for an after ride treat. So far things were going great. Better than Trish and Melissa dreamed of, until Trish looked up to see Davis storming over to her while she was giving her last ride of the day. He looked furious. Trish wondered what was going on and why he was even there, she didn't remember if she mentioned this event to him or not. Whatever it was he looked royally pissed. When he reached her she could see he was struggling to soften the look on his face.

"Daddy! What awe you doing hewe?" the cherub faced little girl Trish held onto in the saddle with her said. "Look daddy I'm widing a howse with Miss Twish! Isn't it pwetty. It's soft too. Miss Twish let me pet him befowe we got on."

"Yes baby I see. I'm glad you're having a good time but I think it's time for us to go. Let's get you down from there and you can go get your cookie and play for a few more minutes with Layla while I talk to Miss Trish." Davis gently lifted Aimee off the horse and sent her on her way. When he turned back to Trish, fury had taken over his face again. "What the hell do you think you're doing? I never gave you permission to put my daughter on the back of this beast. Do you know how dangerous these animals are?

At first Trish was too stunned to speak. Her mouth gaped open in astonishment. As she thought about it, she realized she had made a mistake in assuming that Aimee belonged to the mother and other little girl that had brought her. She had no idea Aimee was Davis' daughter. There must be a million girls named Aimee. Like it or not he had a valid point. It was wrong of her to assume anything when it came to the kids.

She swallowed her pride and said "You're absolutely right. I made a mistake assuming that woman was her mother and therefore I had consent. It never occurred to me to question her parentage. Thank you for showing me I still have some things to work out. I assure you this will never happen again with Aimee or any other child. If you're done screaming at me, I still have other responsibilities to attend to and this horse needs to get back to the stable."

When Davis just glared at her Trish walked the horse back to the barn. She wanted to kick either the horse to go faster or Davis. Definitely Davis as her anger continued to course through her. She felt humiliated and dejected both personally and professionally. She realized just then that

Davis had meant more to her than she had realized and that gave him the power to hurt her. Trish walked up to Melissa and handed her the reins of her horse.

"What was Davis so upset about?" Melissa asked while she took off the horses saddle.

"I gave his daughter a ride without his permission. I didn't realize who she was but I made a mistake in assuming I had permission. Now he's all bent out of shape because he thinks I put his daughter in danger.

Now the relationship was over and she realized she would miss him. It saddened her but she should have known it wouldn't last, as she reminded herself that romance wasn't meant for her. Every once in a while she got a reminder and this was one of those times.

"I'll make an appointment with Larry at the law firm and have a consent form drawn-up before next month's event. As much as I hated to admit it, he had a point about the consent issue. I just wish he could have pointed it out a little more tactfully."

She didn't confide in Melissa how hurt she was by Davis' outburst, or the fact that he had considered her stupid. Though she completely understood why he was upset, it hurt that he thought she would do this intentionally to any child. Maybe this whole charity idea wasn't so great after all. People were funny about their kids. She decided to think about it and talk it over with Melissa. Just because their intentions were good, didn't mean people would be grateful instead of jerks. She would discuss this with Larry too. Try to see it from a different prospective.

Monday morning Trish made an appointment with Larry at the law firm.

She hoped she wouldn't see Davis while she was there but if she did she planned on ignoring him. She wasn't about to let him intimidate her from using the law firm just because he worked there. Besides, it was her law firm long before he had entered her life. The soonest she could get an appointment was Wednesday afternoon.

Wednesday came and went quickly. Time really did fly when you were busy. Trish had a lot to do before the wedding she had organized for Saturday night was all confirmed. The bridezilla had made so many changes that she needed to confirm all the arrangements one last time to be sure everything went off without a hitch. She kept her appointment with Larry, and after speaking with him she felt a lot better about the horseback riding incident she had with Davis. She had Larry work-up a release of liability form and a consent form for future use with her charity. She would also take his suggestion and check into liability insurance as well.

As she was leaving the law office she saw Davis standing at the reception desk. She ignored him and walked past as quickly as possible.

Davis caught a brief glimpse of her as she breezed out the door. "Why was Trish Haywood here?" he questioned the receptionist.

"Oh, she had an appointment with Larry. Something about a release of liability form she needed drawn-up."

Later that day Davis saw Larry in the hallway. "Hey man I saw your lady friend today. Man is she hot. If you ever get tired of her let me know. I wouldn't mind spending some quality time with her if you get my drift. If she's half as fine as she looks I could die a happy man. You're a lucky son of a bitch Davis."

Davis knew he should set Larry straight. Trish Haywood wasn't his. After his outburst at the riding stable, he'd be lucky if she didn't punch him next time he saw her. But something about what Larry said hit a raw nerve in him. Yeah, she didn't show up at the theater last night but he tried to tell himself that she was just busy. He walked by her apartment building after the movie but didn't know which apartment was hers. He would have called but realized he only had her business phone number, so he went home. Disappointment still nagged at him all day today. He still couldn't tell you what movie he had seen. All he could do was think about Trish through the whole damn thing. His pride wouldn't allow him to go to her office and find out where she had been. It was never considered an official date after all. She didn't owe him an explanation. His gut told him that he blew it big time with the horseback riding incident. The question now was how to fix it before some guy like Larry moved in on her.

The thought of some other man putting their lips, or worse yet, their hands on her made him break-out in a sweat. He had some major groveling to do to both Trish and Melissa. Yeah, he could have handled that whole situation a lot better. What surprised him most was that he lost his temper when he had a reputation for keeping his cool in tough situations. He realized almost instantly that he lost his temper because he held Trish to a higher standard than most people, and he did that because he cared about her more than he realized. He kept telling himself he was meeting her at the show because it was a night out, something to kill time until he met someone he wanted to date, but he had found that someone in Trish. He didn't want anyone else. He wanted Trish, mind, body and soul. Davis walked into Celebrations fully prepared to grovel. Melissa sat at her desk typing quickly on her computer and looked up as he approached her desk "Hey Davis, how's it going?" Davis felt the chill in Melissa's voice.

"Good. Listen, I just wanted to apologize about my outburst last Saturday. I could have handled that much better than I did. I'm sorry if I caused you any embarrassment."

"Thanks. I know you were just worried, but it's nice of you to apologize." Melissa's face softened into a slow smile.

"I just want you to know it certainly wasn't intentional. It was a natural assumption that the adult who brought her was her parent." Melissa smiled and said "apology accepted." One down. One to go.

"Is Trish around? I owe her an apology too."

"Sorry. She's already left the office for the day. Do you want to leave a message?"

"No. That's okay, I won't be in the office for the next couple of days. Maybe you could just let her know I apologized to you, and that I'll catch-up with her later. By the way, did she have an appointment last night? I thought I saw her coming out of one of the office buildings down on Main Street but I couldn't catch her." *Liar. Big fat liar.*

"I don't think so. As far as I know she was free last night. She usually goes to the show on Tuesday nights, maybe that's where you saw her?"

"Could be. Thanks. See you later." As he walked out of the office his heart sank to his toes he was so disappointed. He had hoped she hadn't been avoiding him. Now he knew for sure she was. Davis was anxious to get this straightened out. She was all he could think about lately. Too much of a distraction, even when she wasn't around, or maybe more so because she wasn't around. Damn it, he wanted her around. He went back to his office and sulked about it some more. He tried to get some work done, only to be drawn back to thoughts of Trish.

Chapter 5

Trish finished up at the banquet center as the wedding festivities continued in the hall. Overall the wedding went off without any major hitches. Of course there were always the last minute delays. The limo was a little late arriving at the bride's house due to battery trouble. The men's tuxedos were jumbled-up and needed last minute pressing. The usual last minute, unforeseeable things that made life interesting. With the daddy/daughter dance completed Trish's job was done. One quick trip to the ladies room and she was out the door. As she came out of the bathroom Davis grabbed her arm. Startled, Trish looked up, surprised that Davis was even there. She hadn't seen him earlier, and if she had she would have kept out of his way.

"Well, you're a hard person to get a hold of." Davis said.

"I don't know about that. You seem to have a pretty good hold on me now." she tried to free her arm from his grip. He didn't budge as he pulled her closer. "What are you doing here anyway?" She let the irritation she felt show on her face and in her voice.

"The groom works at the law firm. I escorted Aunt Sylvia because Uncle Jake is out of town." Davis answered. "Do you have someplace we could talk in private? Right in here will do." Davis put his arm around her waist and led her into the office she had been working in for the evening. "Did Melissa tell you I stopped by your office on Wednesday?"

"Yes." Trish replied as icily as possible. She had to look away from his piercing blue eyes or she would forget her resolve to stay detached.

"Well, like I told Melissa, I'm sorry for my behavior last Saturday. I could have, and should have, handled it better than I did. Larry told me you were in the office to have those consent and liability forms drawn-up."

"Yes. It was good advice you gave me. I appreciate it." Trish said. "I hope you know I had no idea that Aimee was your

25

Aimee. She seems like a very sweet little girl. I'm sure you're very proud of her." Trish's voice dripped ice as she spoke.

"Really, sometimes I'm so proud I could bust. Now that that's settled, let's move onto to subject number two. You weren't at the theater Tuesday night." Davis turned the conversation to what was really on his mind.

"I know." Trish replied.

So she wasn't going to make this any easier. Fine. We'll do it the hard way. "Was it because you were upset with me?" Davis asked innocently.

"I didn't think it would matter to you one way or the other if I showed up. I'm not good at playing games, so I don't, which is why I don't date. I'm just not good at it." Tears started to threaten Trish's eyes as she blinked hard to keep her emotions in control. She had to get out of there and fast before she started blubbering like a baby.

"It did matter to me that you didn't show up. I missed you. I missed you all week, not just Tuesday night. Are you going stand me up again this week?" Trish looked into his eyes and saw that he was sincere. "Let me rephrase that. Will you please join me at the show this Tuesday? My treat." Davis batted his eyelashes at her. "Better yet, can I come and pick you up? Sort of like a real date. What's your apartment number?"

"Davis I appreciate the apology, I'm sure it wasn't easy, but I don't date. I'm sure you're a nice man and a fun date but I've already told you, dating isn't for me." Trish said firmly.

"Do I stink or have bad breath that you're so repulsed by me that you won't even spend one evening with me? Because I feel the attraction between us and I know you do too. Why are you denying yourself the pleasure of my company when you know you're attracted?"

"Because I'm the type of person that tries to learn something from her mistakes. If I wasn't that type of person I would have never had Larry take care of the consent and liability forms. I've learned from past experiences that dating isn't something I do well so I'm better off not doing it. It's really nothing personal towards you, I'd be saying the same thing to anyone who asked me out."

"But it is personal to me Trish because I want to spend time with you and I wouldn't be putting in so much effort if I wanted someone else. You're special to me and I'm not in the habit of telling women that. I've barely dated since my divorce and you're the first woman I've wanted to spend any time with.

You're real and you don't play games or spend your time trying to manipulate me or the situation to suit you. Please won't you reconsider and if you're not having a good time just let me know and I'll take you right home, no questions asked." Davis realized he was begging now but he didn't care, he wanted her and that was all there was to it.

Trish thought for a moment or two and finally said "Okay. Number 3C. Let's say about seven o'clock?"

Relieved, Davis gently wrapped his arms around Trish and held her in a tender embrace before kissing her. With each kiss the intensity deepened, arousing both of them until passion nearly overcame them. Breathlessly they embraced, desperately clinging to each other. Tongues tangled together as Davis backed Trish against the wall of the small office. His hands began to roam over Trish's slim, sexy body. Her hips thrust up as her back arched into him in response to his caress of her full, firm breasts. Her nipples were taunt against his hands as he plucked and probed over the fabric of her dress. A deep moan escaped Trish's throat as Davis pressed his manhood against her thrusting hips. Every nerve in Trish's body was singing with passion and delight. Lost now, neither one of them had the strength or inclination to stop their burning desire. Until they heard a rather loud, abrupt knock on the open door jam. Larry stood there smiling and slightly embarrassed as he said "Sorry to interrupt but, your Aunt Sylvia is looking for you. I think she's ready to go. What do you want me to tell her?" Larry looked away briefly and cleared his throat, slightly embarrassed but more amused.

"Tell her I'll be right there. Thanks a lot Larry." Davis responded. Larry heard the annoyance in Davis' voice and smiled again as he left the room. Davis was sure he hadn't heard the last of this from Larry.

"I guess I better get going. I'll see you Tuesday, seven o'clock, apartment 3C."

Trish put her hand on Davis' chest and smiled saying "I'm looking forward to it." and watched as he walked out the door.

She had to sit down for a moment to get herself under control. Her legs refused to hold her up any longer as she trembled. Clear thought was impossible. Trish could still feel his hands on

27

her body and his lips on her mouth. She found herself wondering what it would be like if his lips took the place of his hands on her body. *Pure ecstasy*. Never had she thought herself capable of such physical pleasures. Trying to talk herself down from her high, she spoke out loud, "Okay, get a grip". *Down girl. Back to business*. Trish left the office still a little dazed and incredibly happy.

Davis loved his Aunt Sylvia with all his heart but her timing sucked. Or maybe he was lucky she was looking for him, and it was Larry who found them. It wasn't exactly the position he wanted his Aunt to walk in on. He couldn't believe how lost he became in Trish's mouth. He wanted her, and would have taken her, if not for the interruption Larry provided. He wouldn't have cared who was around. She excited him more that any woman he'd been with in a long, long time. He felt like an impatient teenager looking for his first sexual conquest. His head hummed and his body tingled with the mere thought of Trish's body pressed against his. He recalled the way her breasts filled his hands as her hard nipples strained against the fabric of her dress. He was so worked-up he had to stop into the men's room to give himself a chance to get his manhood under control again. Don't think about it. Clear your mind completely of Trish, he thought as he splashed cool water on his face. What he really needed to do was splash cold water on his cock. He wasn't really sure even that would work, but it did sober him enough to feel somewhat in control again.

Chapter 6

By Monday Trish had almost talked herself out of the date on Tuesday night. What was she thinking? Things like this just never worked out for her. She should put a stop to it before she got hurt. It was simply mind over matter. Just because she reacted physically to Davis Sinclair didn't mean she meant anything to him. She should just forget about him.

As Trish boarded the elevator to her office she looked up to see Davis' smiling face. "Good morning. How are you today?" he asked cheerfully.

"Great. How about you?"

"Couldn't be better."

As the elevator became more crowded, Trish and Davis found themselves pushed against the back wall. Davis placed his arm around her waist and pulled her closer to him. He let his hand travel lightly over her back, turning little circles all along her spine with his finger. Trish shuttered in excitement and looked into Davis' smoldering eyes. His hand sensuously caressed her behind, giving it a little squeeze before returning his attention to her back. Trish's knees went weak with excitement as she leaned heavily against Davis for support, pressing the entire length of her body against his. Her breast brushed against his arm with nipples hard as she pressed her hand against his chest to steady herself. Lowering her head she tried to steady her ragged breathing. Davis planted a brief, gentle kiss on the top of her head and she knew that all of her resolve to cancel their date was gone. Trish straightened and looked into Davis' smiling, seductive eyes. She returned the smile as the elevator doors opened and they exited, each one concentrating on their own lustful thoughts. They silently waved goodbye to each other in the hallway and went into their offices.

With a smile on her face, Trish said good morning to Melissa.

"Well, you seem to be in a good mood for a Monday morning. I'm assuming everything went well at the wedding then." Melissa added with a laugh "I saw Larry in the elevator this morning. He mentioned Davis and his aunt were at the wedding. Did you happen to see him?" Melissa asked innocently.

"Larry told you. I tell you he's worse than a woman with his gossip. Tell me what he said." Trish answered.

"Only that apparently you and Davis had 'talked' out your differences and were on 'friendly' terms again." Melissa laughed as she did her air quotation marks. "So tell me your version." she prompted.

"He caught us making-out and groping each other like two teenagers in the back-seat of daddy's car." Trish laughed. "Need I say more?"

"Yeah, how was it? Is he as good as he looks?" She licked her lips and rubbed her palms together.

Trish cleared her throat and answered "Better. If that's at all possible for you to imagine but that's all you're going to get out of me. I don't kiss and tell."

"How about grope and tell?"

"No. Now let's get to work before we both say something we can blackmail each other over."

"Oh man. You're no fun." Melissa handed Trish her messages.

"That's not what Davis says." Trish laughed and walked into her office, closing the door in Melissa's face.

Trish tried to focus on her work but her mind kept drifting back to Davis. *God he's sexy.* She tried not to think about what tomorrow night might bring. She didn't think she was ready to be intimate with him, but then her body seemed to have other ideas whenever she was around him. He made her feel desirable and sexy. She felt like a magnet around him. As if she had no choice but to be drawn to him. Electricity coursed up and down her body with the slightest touch of his hands or his lips. Don't start thinking about those lips, she warned herself. She could spend all day locking lips with him. His kisses could melt the coldest ice maiden. Was this love she was feeling or lust? Lust. How could she even think of love? She'd only known him a few weeks. What kind of idiot was she? She never was one to believe in love at first sight, or second and third sight either. That happed to other people, less sensible people than Trish. She had always prided herself on her level headedness, thoroughly thinking through her decisions. Looking at problems from all angles and being cautious. How could she abandon all her sensibilities for one man? She definitely had to get back on track. Back to the formula that had always worked for her in the past. Tried and true decision making processes. She needed to pull back, away from Davis, she didn't have the capacity to love or be loved. She had never been loved by anyone, ever. Her childhood had been cold and uncaring, being taken care of by the nuns out of obligation. No one ever held her, comforted her when she was sick, lovingly tended to her cuts and scrapes. When she was twenty one and turned out of the convent, no one walked her to the door or even cared if she was there or not, no one was going to be sorry to see her go. No one wished her well. Trish had come to the conclusion long ago that she was unlovable and that was how she still viewed herself today. She visibly shook her head to clear it. She forced Davis Sinclair from her mind and turned her attention to the fund-raising project for the pre-school. *Right.* New playground equipment was the goal. Maybe an indoor carnival would do the trick. She'd run the idea by the chairman of the fund raising committee.

When Davis walked into the reception area Larry jumped-up from his desk where he had been waiting like a hawk ready to attack his prey. "Hey buddy. How's it going? Did you get your Aunt Sylvia home all right the other night? You seemed a little pre-occupied. A little pale, sort of like all the blood had rushed from your head. Are you feeling okay?" He pretended concern while he smiled. "Did you have a good time? That was some wedding. Maybe you overdid it on the dance floor."

"Shut-up Larry and quit laughing" Davis growled. "I'm sure you've been there yourself a time or two before, if you were able to talk some bimbo into it. I heard your date was so blonde she needed someone to read her the instructions on the paper towel dispenser in the ladies room."

"Hey now don't get personal here. Besides, I'm sure I got further with her than you did with Trish. Not that I don't think she's hot. I'd do her any day." Larry said as he wiggled his eyebrows like Groucho Marx.

Suddenly Davis was pissed and showed it briefly to Larry. "Don't talk about Trish like she's a piece of meat being stalked by a lion. She deserves to be treated with more respect than that. She's got brains and she's not a slut."

"Whoa. Settle down buddy. I was just joking around. A little touchy about the little woman I see. Message received. I'll back-off." Larry held up his hands in surrender he turned and left Davis' office.

Maybe Larry had a point. He certainly had a soft spot when it came to Trish. She excited him both physically and intellectually, and he couldn't remember the last time he felt that way about a woman. The thought of touching her soft, creamy skin sent his blood south as he closed his eyes and wallowed in the thought of her. The smell of her stirred his lust for her. He couldn't say it was love. He swore when his ex-wife left him that he would never give himself so completely to another woman. Although to be honest he felt a sense of relief when she was finally gone. She put him through hell with her wild antics and drunken behavior. He would almost say the whole relationship was a mistake, but then he wouldn't have his sweet Aimee.

He was glad he had talked his ex into keeping the baby. She had wanted an abortion, but Davis promised her a lot of money to hold onto the baby and she jumped at it. Yes, in essence he had bought Aimee, but it was the best money he'd ever spent. Truth be told he would have paid her triple what he did for the chance to keep his baby. The day she delivered Aimee was the happiest day of his life. When he gave her the money she signed herself out of the hospital AMA and took-up with some guy from the local motorcycle club. Two days later he brought Aimee home and never looked back. He never regretted his decision to keep Aimee. Not for one minute.

Davis gave his head a quick shake and tried to get back to work. He tried not to think about tomorrow night's date with Trish, but it was useless. She stirred him up this morning on the elevator and he was having trouble settling down. He wondered if she was as riled-up as him. The good news is she never gave him the signal to stop, in fact, just the opposite. There was a lot of passion behind those sapphire blue eyes of hers and he was going to be the one to unleash it. With Trish it was more that the body was willing but the mind was hesitant. And boy what a body she had. Oooh la ,la she was hot. The feel of her silky, smooth hair and soft luminescent skin drove him crazy with desire. The way she melted into his body when he kissed her drove him wild. Caressing her sweet, pert nipples with his hands made his mouth water as he thought about taking them into his mouth. He had to stop thinking about this before he drooled all over the front of his shirt. Luckily, his phone rang and drew him back to reality. Startled, he picked-up the receiver and went back to work.

Chapter 7

Trish agonized over her outfit for the evening. First she thought just jeans and a sweater, but she was feeling a little special tonight. After all, this was their first official date and she wanted to set the right mood. *Well if that were true she'd have to answer the door naked.* She had decided earlier in the day that, although she was unable to love, she couldn't deny herself the physical thrill of being with a man, specifically Davis. Never had she felt so wanted, even needed, as she did when she was in his arms and she liked the feeling. So she was going to go with it and just let it take her where it may. Trish wouldn't allow herself to feel guilty by helping it along with the right outfit. Something casual, but sexy. After some thought, Trish decided on a pair of brown skinny jeans topped off with a very sexy, clinging lace camisole in a rich cream color. Over the camisole she put on a very sheer cream colored peasant blouse that had a satin tie at the v-neck, which she left untied. She wore her hair down and finished the look with a pair of knee high brown boots with spike heels. While she nervously brushed her hair for the third time the doorbell rang. With knots in her stomach she took a deep nervous breath, smiled and opened the door. Expecting to see Davis she startled as she saw her friend and down-the-hall neighbor Candy.

"Hi stranger, I haven't seen you in like forever! Where have you been hiding yourself lately? Wow, you look great by the way, hot outfit." Candy breezed through the door. "I got invited to a party on the fourth floor and stopped by to see if you wanted to hang out tonight. Interested?"

"Sorry not tonight. I have a date." Trish paused as she let the information sink into Candy's brain.

"Wait a minute, am I hearing right? Miss 'I don't have a romantic bone in my body'. Miss 'I'm done with dating because it just never works out for me' actually has a date with a real, live man? He's not inflatable is he?" Candy laughed at her own joke. "Tell me all about him. What's his name? What does he do for a living? Where did you meet him? Come on. Spill it."

The knock at the door startled them both.

"See for yourself and be *Nice*!" Trish opened the door and smiled at Davis' reaction. His gaze heated instantly when he saw her and, just as quickly, passed as he noticed Candy.

Mission accomplished. His eyes had nearly bugged out of his head when he'd seen her.

Davis looked so handsome in his dark denim jeans and light blue denim shirt. He wore the collar of the button down shirt open and, peeking beneath it, was a dark navy crew neck shirt. He smelled remarkable! She felt the electricity sizzle in the air as she invited him in with a warm smile on her sensuous lips.

"Hey handsome, how's it going? I'd like you to meet my friend and neighbor, Candy. Candy, this is Davis Sinclair."

They nodded to each other and said hello. Candy's eyes crossed in a yummy expression as she looked at Trish and said her goodbye.

"Call me." Candy called back to Trish as she strolled down the hall.

Turning, she found herself pressed against Davis in a warm embrace. He kissed her, gently at first, then intensified the kiss as he tightened his arms around her small, soft waist. She stroked his neck as she played with his hair.

All thoughts of time and space faded away as Trish surrendered to the sensations her body was experiencing and enjoying. Her eyes closed as she let out a soft moan of pure pleasure and passion while they kissed each other with increased fervor. Their tongues met and tangled as they explored and plunged into each other's mouth in an erotic dance. Davis trailed his kisses along her jaw and nibbled gently on her ear as he worked his way slowly, sensually down her neck. Trish's body tingled and zinged, her nipples hardened into excited pebbles as he moved his way down her neck. Trish let out a little giggle as he reached the base of her neck.

"Sorry. Just a little ticklish there." she murmured. Reluctantly, Davis slowly released her and slightly, very slightly, stepped back.

"Nice to know where your ticklish spots are, do you have any more?" Davis asked.

"That's for me to know and you to find out" Trish laughed. She gave him a suggestive wiggle of her eyebrows.

"Can't wait. By the way, have I mentioned how fantastic you look?"

"No, I don't think so," Trish answered. "Let me just grab my cell phone and I'll be ready to go."

Davis looked around her apartment while he waited. It was small and clean. Not fussy or cluttered. Simple, with little accents of color scattered around the room. One entire wall contained floor to ceiling bookshelves that were almost completely filled with, what else, books. Most people had a few books and knick knacks scattered around. She obviously liked to read. *Romance novels?* She liked romance novels? He was surprised. Stunned actually. Trish was so down to earth he would have thought she went for the classics.

 The walls were painted a calming green, more of a gray-green really, with white accents. Her couch added a punch of color with its multi-colored floral pattern and classic in its design. The two chairs she had were in a complimentary gingham check to the couch, giving the room a comfy, homey feeling. Two end tables on each end of the couch matched the oak mission styled television cabinet that sat across from the couch.

"Oh, I see you've found out about my other secret passion. Reading." Trish said.

"Yeah. I like to read too, just not romance novels."

"You call them romance novels. I call them self-help books. You'd be amazed what you can learn from them."

"Really? Tell me all about it."

"Okay, but I'd rather show you instead. As you can see I read a lot. It could take a very long time to show you everything." She took his hand and walked him to the door. "I'm ready to go. What kind of movie do you feel like seeing tonight?" She looked at him, and with a mutual understanding they both started to laugh. Neither one of them had actually watched a movie since they started meeting at the theater. There was no reason to think anything would be different tonight. But yet it was different. This was a date. This felt more official and much more exciting. This evening sizzled and sparked with unrestrained passion and anticipation of things to come.

"What do you feel like seeing" Davis asked as they read the marquee.

"I hate to say it, but I've seen all of them already."

"That's o.k. you look too luscious to sit in the dark anyway. Do you like blues music? There's this little blues joint that Larry told me about. It's called Moody's and I think it's just up the block a little, if that's o.k. with you?"

"Sounds great. I've heard about it but I've never been there before. Lead the way."

Davis took her hand and they walked and talked as they meandered their way lazily to the club. Moody's was exactly the right name for the club. When they first entered it was dark and a little hazy as they blinked, trying to adjust their eyes to the darkness. Quaint little wooden bistro tables were scattered throughout the room in what looked like a random order. Most of them were two-seaters and all of them offered a clear view of the stage. The tables had a very rustic, used look to them, as did the matching chairs. The walls were painted a dark navy blue except for the stage wall, which was painted a kind of dirty cream color. The ceiling was also navy blue with black fans mounted throughout the room that lazily spun their blades in slow steady circles. Spotlights were mounted between the fans and were pointed at the stage. Along the back wall the bar stretched the entire length of the wall. The wooden front was well worn and scuffed but clean. Round backless vinyl stools lined the front of the bar. The rustic atmosphere made one feel that they had been transported back to the bayou. Very quaint and cozy. Just the type of place where lovers could sit and cuddle, whispering intimately into each other's ear. Dark enough where you could remain anonymous and no one cared. Davis lead Trish to a table in the corner by the stage. The waitress came to take their order.

"What can I get you folks tonight?" Davis motioned to Trish to order first. "I'll have a ginger ale, light ice." Davis ordered a Molson and the waitress hurried off to fill their order.

"You sure you don't want something stronger than ginger ale, maybe a root beer?" Davis teased.

"No thanks. I don't drink alcohol. It doesn't agree with me. Besides, I can have a good time without it so what's the point?"

Davis could respect that. He liked a beer once in a while but that was about the extent of it, unlike Aunt Sylvia and Uncle Jake. Cocktails were served promptly at six thirty every night without fail.

As luck would have it tonight was open mike night with quite a variety of entertainment. Some even came to do some stand-up comedy and Davis and Trish found themselves continually entertained as they held hands under the table. Davis sat with his arm around the back of Trish's chair as he lightly caressed her arm. Occasionally they kissed each other leisurely. Davis enjoyed and savored the taste and sensations that stirred within him. Anticipation sizzled through him while he lightly caressed her with his hands and lips. It left him feeling a little giddy and dizzy at the same time. They stayed at the club until the entertainment stopped, well after midnight. He held his arm around her as they walked back to her apartment to help ward-off the chill in the air.

They enjoyed a passionate kiss-fest at the door to her apartment. Trish even considered inviting him in but decided she better quit thinking with the wrong part of her anatomy. She needed to keep playing it safe for a little while longer.

"Thanks Davis for a great evening. I really had a good time." Trish breathed raggedly, trembling as she spoke.

"You sound a little surprised that you enjoyed yourself."

"To be honest, I don't usually like dating but tonight was really an unexpected pleasure. You're really fun to hang around with, I find you exciting both physically and mentally. Really, really good physically." She laid her hands on his muscular chest and slowly ran them down to his waist. "I'll talk to you later." Trish turned and vanished into her apartment quickly before she changed her mind. Never in her life had she ever been so attracted to a man.

Davis found himself smiling the rest of the way home. Trish was awesome. Funny. Smart. Kind. Very feminine. Soft. Sexy, sexy, and more sexy. Her sweet, soft lips were a wonder to explore. She stirred him to his very core as he remembered their passionate embraces and electrifying kisses. He wanted to taste her, touch her, excite her, pleasure her. He felt consumed by her, and he found he liked the feeling. He definitely had to see her again, and soon. She was getting under his skin like an itch that couldn't get scratched.

Chapter 8

Davis didn't sleep very well that night with all his thoughts turning to Trish and his fantasies of what they could do together. Masturbation didn't help. It wasn't just about the orgasm as much as the lust he felt for her. The craving of his body to be touched and caressed by her long slender fingers with their sexy French manicure consumed him. How would those hands look wrapped around his hard cock? The thought of her mouth on his body licking, nipping, sucking and kissing making him moan loudly. He forced himself out of bed and back to reality. He showered then rinsed in ice cold water. That didn't work either.

He had breakfast with Aimee as she told him all about her day yesterday. He smothered his laughter as she told him about how icky boys were and how she was sure they were there just to aggravate her cause they were just too gross to believe. The fact that she said her r's like w's made the story that much more adorable. The word gross came out like 'gwoss'. She held nothing back as she told her stories with the innocence of a child. She was his miracle. The fact that he had to marry her mother just to insure her survival didn't detract at all from the love he felt for her. It was worth every minute and every dollar he had to sacrifice to see her beautiful little face every morning.

Davis went to work and stopped at the florist in the lobby of the building and bought a dozen red roses with baby's breath for Trish. He took one rose out and ordered the rest delivered to her office. The note enclosed said simply:

Last night was heaven.
For the rest of your bouquet, come to my office anytime.
Davis

Trish sat at her desk preparing a presentation. She was so absorbed in her work she didn't hear Melissa come in. When she heard Melissa clear her throat she looked up to see the beautiful bouquet of roses Melissa was holding. In her other hand was a card.

"So what have you been doing to earn flowers?" Melissa asked.

"I'm not sure, but let's read the card and see." Trish opened the card and read it, then handed it to Melissa to read.

"You went out with him? Why didn't you tell me? Cough it up. I want details, now."

Trish filled her in with all the details, even the crack she made about the romance books being self-help books.

"Oh god, it sounds hot between you two. I've been to Moody's a couple of times. It's so raw and romantic there. So when are you seeing him again?"

"Apparently today if I want to rescue the rest of my flowers. I guess now is as good a time as any. Hold down the fort." Trish walked out the door, straightening her outfit and smoothing her hair nervously. Anticipation consumed her with excitement at the thought of seeing Davis.

Since she didn't know which office Davis occupied she had to stop at the reception desk to ask. Just her luck Larry happened to be standing there at the time.

"Hey Trish, what brings you here?"

"I'm here to see Davis but I don't know which office is his."

"No problem. I'll personally escort you. It's good for my image to be seen with beautiful women. Keeps the ladies talking, you know. Come with me." Larry knocked on the door.

"Come in." Davis answered.

"Special delivery!" Larry opened the door for Trish. She walked into his office slowly as she peeked her head around the door. He sat behind a large mahogany desk that screamed authority. Behind him were matching bookshelves with a small scattering of knick knacks distributed among the shelves, and large, heavy leather bound books neatly lined up and arranged by color. Sitting in front of the desk were two black leather chairs. Along the wall with the door sat a matching black leather sofa and a coffee table that matched the mahogany of the desk. His office was testosterone heaven and it suited him perfectly. The only things that hung on the walls were his diplomas from both U of M and Harvard Law School. *Wow, he went to Harvard?*

"I'll just leave you two love birds alone" Larry discretely closed the door behind him.

"Hi. I hope I'm not interrupting. I just got the flowers Davis. Thank you so much, they're really beautiful."

Davis came around to the front of the desk and took her into his arms, kissing her as she looked up into his handsome face. Her heart flipped more times than a gymnast doing her floor routine at the Olympics. Never had she had such a physical response to a man's touch.

"You're welcome, but their nowhere near as beautiful as you. I was hoping it was you at the door. I can't stop thinking about you."

"Well if it's any consolation I'm right there with you, I can't seem to concentrate on my own name today. What are you doing to me Mr. Sinclair? Whatever it is, don't stop." Davis kissed her again deeper, harder and more demanding than before, adding lust to the dizzying mixture of lips and tongue. He gave her bottom lip a little nip as he ended the kiss.

"I wanted to ask you to a little costume party Larry is giving this Saturday night at his place. Do you have any events planned for Saturday night?"

"I'd love to go. I only have a baby shower planned in the afternoon. What time were you thinking?"

"About eight?"

"Yeah, sounds like a lot of fun. I've never been to a costume party before. Is this adult's only or is it a family thing? I wouldn't want to corrupt any innocents with my costume." and she wiggled her eyebrows and laughed.

"Adults only, Larry isn't very kid oriented."

"What costume are you wearing? I wouldn't want us to wear the same thing."

"I'm not telling, but I guarantee you won't be wearing the same one I am." Davis' phone buzzed and he pressed the interoffice button.

"Mr. Sinclair your appointment is here." Terri, his receptionist, announced.

"Great. I'll be right there. May I see you to the door? Oh! I almost forgot to give you this." He handed her the single long-stemmed, red rose to complete her bouquet.

She went up onto her tip toes and kissed him sweetly on the lips. "Yes. And thank you again for the beautiful flowers." Trish had to keep reminding herself not to touch him in the hallway. The urge to hold his hand was hard to resist. Davis opened the outer door for her and gave a slight bow.

"Bye" he whispered. Trish gave a low wave goodbye as she sniffed the rose, smiling back over her shoulder at him.

Trish paced her living room nervously as she waited for Davis. She was having second thoughts about her Cat Woman costume. It was from the Hallie Berry version, not the old Batman series. It was so form fitting that it showed everything god had given her, even though it covered her from neck to ankle. Lucky for her it had a built-in bra but she had to go commando on the lower half because her thong lines showed. She wore a mask that showed her blue eyes but continued down her face to the tip of her nose, and she accented her lips with hot, red lipstick. The little cat ears peeked above the skull cap that covered Trish's hair half-way down her head and all of her forehead. Trish didn't know how long she could tolerate the mask, it was pretty hot to wear but the spandex of the body suit made that part at least comfortable to wear. She added black, spike-heeled boots to finish the look.

Davis knocked on the door and Trish immediately burst out laughing when she saw costume. Fred Flintstone, club and all. He even messed-up his dark brown hair to give a rugged effect. The costume suited him perfectly. Trish could see the outline of his muscular arms through the flesh-toned cloth that clung to them. The furry animal covering came just above his knees. *Nice legs.* The only alteration he made to the outfit, were the sandals he wore.

Davis' eyes bugged out of his head when he saw Trish. All the blood from his head rushed to his groin and his heart did flip-flops over and over again.

"You look amazing! I always wanted my own little pussy-cat. I can't wait to make you purr for me. Are you ready to go? Is there a cape or something you need to cover-up with? It's a little chilly outside."

"Are you afraid to be seen with me? It's a little more revealing than I thought. Do you think it's too much?" Suddenly she was a little more unsure about her choice.

"No. I'm just afraid I'm going have to spend the whole night using my club on all the other men at the party. I personally love it."

"Davis, believe me when I tell you that the other men can look, but I'll never leave any doubt in their minds that I'm there with you, and that I have every intention of leaving with you. I have no interest in any of those other men. I only have eyes for you…no pun intended." She kissed him strongly on the mouth as she wrapped her leg around his hip and pressed the length of her body against his. The fuck me boots she wore were already coming in handy.

When they got to Larry's house the party was already in full swing and had started to overflow from the house into the back yard where he had a D.J. set-up and a portable dance floor down.

"Trish! I didn't know you were coming tonight." Trish turned to see Melissa in a giant crab costume.

"Melissa? I didn't know you were coming either."

"I like your costume but, honestly, I don't think too many people want to leave with crabs." Trish joked.

"Did you come with someone, because with an outfit like that you're guaranteed to leave with anyone you want." Melissa commented with a wink and a not.

Trish raised her eyebrows and laughed.

"I came with Davis and I intend on leaving with Davis."

Davis walked up to the two women and handed Trish her coke.

"Don't tell me I'll have to use my club on some of the women here too. I was taught not to hit girls…. hard, anyway. Hey Melissa, how's it going?" He slipped his free arm around Trish's waist and pulled her a little closer, then took her hand to hold. He wasn't taking any chances. He wanted everyone to know exactly who she belonged with.

"Did you come with someone Melissa?" Trish wanted to know.

"No. I thought I'd play the field. There's some mighty fine looking men around here and I intend on talking to all of them before the night is over."

"Let me give you a little tip Melissa." Davis leaned in and whispered "I work with the guy in the Popeye outfit over there and those muscles are fake." Davis laughed.

"Okay. Good to know. Thanks for the info. Well, good to see you two. I have to start circulating. So many men, so little time. Such is life." She dashed back into the house.

Davis led Trish out into the backyard where they talked with so many people that worked with Davis she started having trouble keeping them straight. Finally the D.J. played a slow song, I Only Have Eyes For You , and Davis asked Trish to dance.

43

Alone at last, they settled into each other's arms and swayed with the music.

"We fit good together Haywood."

"I have to agree with you on that Sinclair." Trish rested her head on his shoulder and softly kissed his neck. She closed her eyes and enjoyed all the sensations coursing through her body. Yeah, she was into Davis Sinclair up to her eyeballs. Trish tried not to panic at the thought, pushing her fears to the back of her mind. She took in the cool, clean scent of him and decided to enjoy the moment. Her body was humming like a beehive about to explode.

The partygoers began to thin out quite a bit as Davis and Trish danced, seemingly in their own little world. When Trish finally looked up she realized it was probably time to go. With some regret Trish released her hold on Davis and began to look for Larry to say good night. Trish was surprised to see that Melissa was still there. Melissa had never struck her as a party animal.

"Wow Melissa I didn't know you were still here." Apparently she had gotten smart and ditched the crab costume and was now dressed in a red turtleneck and black mini skirt. *Much better.*

"Yeah, um, Larry asked me to stay a little while. I told him I'd help him clean-up a little." Melissa said with a suggestive smile. Trish got the message loud and clear.

"I get it. Goodnight. See you Monday."

When they got in the car Davis asked "Okay, you want to tell me what you and Melissa really talked about, because I know all of that was in 'woman talk' mumbo jumbo."

"Sure, I'll translate. Her and Larry were really hitting it off and she was staying, hopefully the whole night, if you get my drift." Trish winked.

"You got all that from two sentences?"

"Yeah."

"What about me? Am I getting lucky tonight?" Davis wiggled his eyebrows up and down and smiled.

"Maybe. I need to tell you something first, and then I'll leave the decision up to you."

"Deal" he said eagerly. "What is it?" He already knew his decision. *Woo Hoo!! Tonight's my lucky night!*

"If I sleep with you, it would be with the expectation that you won't be with anyone else while we're together. I need a commitment of fidelity."

"Baby, I'm all yours and I would expect the same from you."

"So you'll tell me before you go out with someone else?" Trish pressed on.

"Right now that's the furthest thing from my mind, but yeah."

"One more thing, I've never been intimate with a man before. You'd be my first." Trish was embarrassed. She was glad they were in the darkness of the car so she didn't have to see the look on his face.

"I know most men would expect a twenty eight year-old to be experienced, so if it's a turn-off I understand. Like I said it's up to you."

"You'd give yourself to me?" Davis asked with disbelief. This complicated things. He was flattered and scared at the same time. His palms began to sweat.

"Yes." she said simply. Embarrassed, she turned and looked out the window with her hands folded in her lap. She waited for him to speak for what seemed like an eternity.

Davis gently took her hand and raised it to his lips and kissed each finger. "I'm honored and humbled that you trust me enough to give yourself to me. You know the first time for a woman can be hard, but I'll do my very best to make it as enjoyable for you as possible. Deal?"

"Deal. Do we shake hands now? After all, you're the lawyer here." Trish smiled and she felt relief and fear at the same time. She hadn't realized she had been holding her breath until she let it out. Her emotions and hormones were in a jumbled frenzy, but as she looked into Davis' eyes she saw calm. He stroked her wrist with his thumb as he tried to reassure her. "It'll be beautiful because you're beautiful, inside and out. I hope you know I care about you. That it's not just sex to me." He tried to reassure her.

"I feel the same about you Davis or I wouldn't even consider this."

Davis parked the car in front of Trish's apartment. He leaned over and kissed her gently, knowing she was probably pretty nervo

45

Chapter 9

Back at Larry's house, Melissa was making the rounds with a large black trash bag collecting all the trash she could find. Larry was in the kitchen loading the dishwasher. He was pretty tired but very pleased that his party had been a success. He really felt too tired to clean-up but he knew he'd be glad in the morning, or if he had his way, mid-afternoon at the earliest if Melissa was cooperative.

"Well I think I got all the trash. I shut-off the patio lights and closed and locked the doors. It looks good in here too. I'm sure some of your furniture has been moved around but I don't know where it goes so I'll leave that to you. So I guess I'll take-off." she said tiredly. "I never did find my costume so if you find it you can just bring it into the office."

Larry stopped doing dishes and turned to her "Are you gonna be crabby now cause you lost your costume?"

"Very funny. I guess I deserved all the wise cracks tonight. I don't know what I was thinking on that one. Well, thanks for inviting me."

Larry abruptly took her into his arms and kissed her boldly several times. When he felt her arms go around his neck to tighten the embrace he deepened the kiss as he probed her opening mouth with his tongue. They simultaneously quickened the pace as their bodies became a jumble of flying clothes and probing hands, their urgency pushing them faster and faster. Larry explored Melissa's body, lingering on her exposed breasts with his tongue and hands at the same time. Melissa arched her back and took his cock in her hands, feeling his hardness as she caressed his balls. They both groaned with pleasure as his fingers entered her and brought her quickly to climax. He entered her without waiting for her shuttering to subside and pumped into her, slowly at first, until she yelled breathlessly.

"Faster. Harder."

Without hesitation he did as he was told, pumping into her hard and fast as they both climaxed together on the kitchen floor, collapsing into each other's arms.

"Wow." Melissa breathed. "You really got the moves there Larryman." Melissa looked around the kitchen as she struggled to catch her breath.

"Shit. We made another mess in the kitchen." Melissa laid there and took in the jumble of clothes strewn around the room.

"Let's go make another mess in my bedroom." Larry stood up and grabbed Melissa's hand, helping her up off the floor he led her to his bedroom. Melissa followed gladly as Larry led the way, stopping every once in a while and kissing Melissa.

"Do you think Davis and Trish are doing the wild thing tonight too?" Melissa wondered out loud.

"If there's a god they are. Davis has it bad for her, that's for sure. You practically need a cattle prod to get his attention around the office."

"Same here. I've never seen Trish so happy before, I hope she stays that way. Davis isn't the type to love 'em and leave 'em is he? I mean, I would hate to see her get hurt, she's pretty innocent when it comes to men."

"Davis is a good guy. He'll do right by her." he reassured. "Now me, I'm the horniest toad you'll ever meet, so breaks over little lady. Hop to it."

They laughed as they fell onto Larry's unmade bed and into each other's arms.

As soon as the door to Trish's apartment was closed, Davis pressed Trish against it and kissed her firmly on the mouth. She parted her lips as an invitation that he readily accepted, thrusting his tongue into her mouth as their tongues began a fervent duel. Time stood still as they lingered on a sea of pleasure, moving their hands over each other's bodies through the cloth of their costumes. Davis' fingers found the top of the zipper to her costume and very slowly lowered it, all the while kissing and lightly nipping at her pouty, swollen lips. He slid the costume down so that it pooled around her waist and freed her arms to continue her exploration of his hard, taunt body. She lifted his costume over his head and tossed it on the floor as he cupped her firm breasts. She looked down and burst out laughing, his boxers matched the animal print of his costume.

"What? I don't do anything half assed you know." He kissed her then moved his mouth seductively down her neck as his hands found her pert, hardened nipples. He let his mouth take over where his hands left off as he sucked her rosy hard nipples, caressing them with his tongue and lightly nipping at the hardened tips. Trish's legs weakened as she fought to stay standing, arching her back and moaning loudly as Davis plunged his mouth from one breast to the other. Her more than ample breasts spilled over the top of his hands as he kneaded them while he suckled his way down and around her lean, soft body. Her skin was so soft and silky as he nipped and sucked, leaving little marks of passion as he moved his mouth over every inch of her. He continued to hold her breast in one hand while he explored with his other hand. Suddenly he lifted Trish into his arms and carried her to the bedroom. He gently laid her on the bed. He stood there for a moment taking in her beauty before he began to take her boots off. He pulled her body suit down over her curvaceous hips, caressing as he went down the length of her body until it was completely off. He kissed his way slowly back up her body, lingering behind her knees where she was most sensitive. When he reached her thighs he realized with a shock that she wasn't wearing any underwear, not even a thong. The thought made him dizzy with excitement, his cock jolting impatiently.

"You didn't wear any underwear tonight?"

"No. I couldn't wear any because the panty lines showed so I decided to go without."

Davis smiled broadly. Lucky for Trish she hadn't shared that information with him earlier or he would have ravaged her in the backseat of his car like a teenager. He stood there staring at her, admiring her body through the golden glow of the night light that shone into the bedroom from the attached bathroom. He laid down next to her and sighed.

"You're perfect, just perfect." He rolled her onto her stomach and began his exploration all over again, first with his hands and then with his mouth. He reached around and played with one of her breasts as he kissed and nipped his way down her spine. Now they were both moaning as Davis caressed her core. She was so wet, so ready. He bent one of her knees as he teased her with his broad hand, cupping her curly mound and massaging her with his palm before gently putting a finger inside her. A groan escaped her as he found her sweet clit, in no time at all she was pumping her hips as she rode his finger.

Trish was near frenzy as he worked his finger in and out while she helplessly pumped her hips. Desperately she tried to gain the release she craved. When her climax exploded through her she screamed in delight. Never had she expected such a forceful, fulfilling release to rock her body. Her entire being throbbed and pulsed, quivering with excitement while little tremors continued to explode throughout her body. Davis waited a beat to let her settle before he began to work her again with his fingers. Trish was stunned at her body's instant reaction to his touch. Again Trish felt the rise of her excitement. Every nerve in Trish's body was screaming as the mounting tension built, layer upon layer, until she was ready to explode. She yelled as the next climax overtook her, making her shake and shutter with pleasure.

Davis poised over her spread legs as he prepared to enter her heat.

"You're sure about this? I can stop if I have to." *Please god, don't make me stop!*

"Take me Davis, please! I can't take any more!" Trish panted as she pulled him down to her and gave herself to him. He slowly entered her until he felt her maiden's veil and, as he broke through the barrier he covered her mouth with his.

"You okay baby? The worst part is over and it will get better. I promise, baby."

She nodded yes and smiled as she opened her eyes to gaze up at him. He began to move again, slowly, gently, until she fell into his gentle rhythm and rocked her hips to meet his thrusts. He gradually increased his speed and intensity as they both began to breathe heavily. A light blush spread over her cheeks as Davis thrust into her. She had never looked as lovely as she did right now. Flush with the beauty of their love making. Matching him thrust for thrust he felt her tight muscles clinch and release, sucking his heavy cock as he spilled his seed in her with such force he thought it would never end. Davis looked at Trish, her eyes filled with tears as the slid down into her hair.

"Oh, god. Did I hurt you? I'm so sorry." Davis asked in a panic. Trish gently placed her hand over his mouth to quiet him.

49

"It was soooo beautiful, except, there are no words to describe it. Incredible. Magnificent. Thank you for giving this to me. I'm so happy right now, I'm overwhelmed." Trish sniffed "And now I just feel like a fool for crying so I'll get a grip now."

"Oh baby you are so incredible. Magnificent. Beautiful. I'm humbled by you." Davis took her into his arms and kissed her gently over and over until they both fell asleep.

Chapter 10

Trish woke with a start, forgetting where she was for a moment. Oh yeah. Now she remembered. She was in her bed with Davis - wait- where was Davis? She sat up and looked around as she realized he wasn't in bed with her. She sat for a minute and listened, realizing the shower was running. For a moment she wondered if she had dreamt it all. She got out of bed and walked into the open door of the bathroom.

"Davis, are you alright?" He pulled back the shower curtain as the water dripped into his eyes.

"Oh man I woke you. Sorry. Just thought I'd clean-up here before I go home. Do you mind?"

Trish moved o him. He suddenly grabbed her and pulled her into the spray of the shower and embracing her tightly. She squeaked in delight as he kissed her.

"But it's still dark out. You really have to go?" She wanted him to stay and cuddle with her in her warm bed.

"Unfortunately, I still have a little girl to get home to. Sunday's are daddy/daughter day at my house and Josie's day off. I don't want to have to answer a bunch of four year-olds questions about where daddy was and how come his hair's wet and how come his bed is made so early in the morning."

"Oh, gosh. I forgot all about Aimee. Of course you're right, absolutely. Can I make you some coffee or something to eat?"

"No, no. I'm good. I'll probably go back to sleep when I get home, someone kept me up all night making love." He teased her.

"You know I would never have guessed you were a screamer during climax." He laughed as her face flushed with embarrassment.

"I wouldn't know, I was drowned out by someone else's yelling." She shot back.

"I see someone's still up." Trish caressed his erect manhood. She loved the smooth silky feel over the steel hardness of his erect cock.

She kissed her way down his body as she went to her knees and tentatively put her mouth on his manhood

"Tell me if I do it wrong. I've only read about it." She began her glorious assault on him. He moaned over and over in pleasure as her mouth explored him and her hands caressed his muscled body. She found she was enjoying herself more than she ever expected. She cupped his sac and held his backside as she took him all the way into her mouth and sucked firmly on him as her tongue worked his sensitive tip. Davis put his hands on her head and held her there while he moaned and panted. When he climaxed they both moaned with pleasure, reluctant to let go of each other.

"Was that o.k.? Did I do it right?" She kissed her way back up his body, finally meeting his lips.

"Oh, baby, that was more than all right. Awesome. Perfect. You're fantastic Trish." He held her against him for as long as possible, not wanting to leave her. When they both started to shiver from the cold water now pouring over them Trish looked up into his adoring eyes.

"You better get going. It's starting to get light out."

Trish laughed hysterically when Davis came out of the bathroom with his costume on.

"It's all I had to wear. I guess I could have planned this a little better. I hope I don't get stopped by the cops on the way home. Oh, I realized I don't have your cell phone number and you don't have mine. Can we exchange?"

"Sure. Just don't give it out to anybody okay? You and Melissa are the only two people who have it and I'd like to keep it that way."

"No problem. You give me your phone and I'll give you mine and we'll program each other's."

They exchanged phones and Trish walked him to the door. They lingered over a passionate kiss before he walked out the door. When she looked down at her phone she laughed. Instead of putting his name in her phone listing he put 'World's Greatest Lover' and then his phone number. Trish turned on the television and went into the bedroom to get Davis' pillow to sleep on in front of the television set. She could still smell his glorious scent as she drifted off to sleep while she remembered their time together. Completely content and more relaxed than she had ever been in her entire life.

When Trish woke-up it was nearly one in the afternoon. She felt a wonderful tenderness between her legs as she lazily stretched on the couch, remembering the glory of the previous night. Davis had been fantastic with her. He was so caring, loving actually, as if he really cared for her. Funny, she didn't feel any guilt about what she and Davis had done. What they had done was beautiful, natural even. Those poor nuns that raised her had no idea what they were missing. Being raised her entire life at the convent really did a number on her psyche. Today was going to be a good day and she wasn't going to ruin it with her painful memories of the convent.

Trish showered and made breakfast – okay, she only had some yogurt but it still counted. It was such a sunny fall day she decided to take a long walk in the park. She took some stale bread to feed to the ducks at the big pond in the center of the park. The leaves on the trees danced in the sunlight as all their vibrant colors combined to make her eyes stare in amazement. People were out in force as they realized that this might be one of the last nice days of fall before the winter winds began to blow. Kayakers paddled around the big pond while skaters pushed past her as she walked and absorbed the warm rays of the sun. Trish took a seat on one of the benches, content to just sit and people watch. It was one of her favorite pastimes. A couple she guessed to be well into their eighties sat on a bench down the way, holding hands lovingly. Children ran around in the thick bed of leaves that had already fallen from the trees, laughing in delight at the crunching noise they made. These were the reasons that fall was one of Trish's favorite time of year. Her phone rang, playing the chicken dance ring tone. She loved the chicken dance because it always made her laugh. She looked at the display, which read World's Greatest Lover and giggled to herself.

"Hello."

"Hey there how's my girl?" Davis asked.

"Great. Glorious. Happy. Blissfully happy. And how is my man?"

"Feeling fine and looking even better. What are you up to today?"

"Well, right now I'm at the park enjoying this beautiful day and as soon as I get to the pond I'm going to feed the ducks a loaf of bread I brought along with me.

"Sounds like a plan. Actually, Aimee and I are in the park too. She's playing on the playground. Would you like to meet us at the Gazebo and we can all feed the ducks together, that is if you're willing to share your stale bread with us."

"Sounds great. Is Aimee almost done on the playground or do you need more time?"

'Believe me, when I tell her she gets to feed the ducks she'll be ready to leave the playground. Meet you there in five minutes."

"Okay." She changed direction and headed back toward the Gazebo. When Trish approached the Gazebo Aimee came running to her.

"Miss Twish! Daddy said I get to feed the ducks! Awe you gonna come with us?" She was so excited she was jumping up and down and grabbing Trish's hand to start pulling her toward the pond.

"Did you bring your howse with you? I like your howse."

"Hi Aimee! No, I didn't bring the horse today. The horse is taking a nap today. So you're going to help me feed the ducks today? I really appreciate the help, there are so many of them and I don't want to forget anyone."

Trish looked up to Davis' smiling blue eyes. He kissed her thoroughly but briefly, then gently caressed her cheek.

"Hey, beautiful." Davis said simply, as his eyes spoke volumes he couldn't find the words to express. Softly, lovingly conveying the tenderness he was feeling toward Trish.

Trish smiled back at Davis.

"I know what you mean." Trish simply grabbed his hand and gave it a brief squeeze, then turned her attention back to Aimee. They all walked to the pond together and fed the ducks. The ducks made happy sounds as they gobbled-up the bread that Aimee fed them. Aimee's squeals of joy had everyone around them chuckling as her non-stop jabbering delighted Trish and Davis. Aimee loved the ducks but was also a little afraid of them, but she never let it stop her.

She's a gutsy little thing. Aimee searched the bag thoroughly until every last crumb was dispensed. When she walked away from the edge of the pond all the ducks began to follow her, looking for more food. That freaked her out a little and she ran behind Davis to hide from them, quietly peering around his legs to see if they were still there. Satisfied that they had given up their quest for food, Aimee came back in front of Davis and took his hand in hers. Her hand was so tiny compared to Davis'.

"Well I guess it's time for me to go" Trish said "I have some work to do at home that I've put off long enough." Trish stooped down to look into Aimee's eyes. "Thank you so much for helping me today, Aimee. I don't know what I would have done without you."

Suddenly Aimee's arms were around her neck and she gave Trish a big raspberry on her right cheek and then covered that with a kiss. Trish hugged her gently and kissed her little chubby cheek. She was such a sweet little girl with her curly brown hair and big brown eyes. She was petite and just the right weight for her small frame. Her face was something Trish imagined Da Vinci would have painted with her cherub like features. Trish wondered what her mother looked like, although she could see Davis in her mouth and the shape of her eyes, she definitely had some of her mother's features.

"Awen't you gonna kiss daddy goodbye?" Aimee asked so sweetly.

"Absolutely, I'm going to kiss daddy goodbye." Trish smiled and kissed Davis on the lips lightly.

"No, you did it wong, you have to give waspbewwies first THEN you kiss his lips."

"Oh, boy. Do you think I should try it again?" Trish asked Aimee with concern.

Aimee nodded her head yes and watched intently as Trish did it to her satisfaction.

"Okay. That's bettew. Daddy it's youw tuwn to kiss Miss Twish."

Davis raspberried Trish's cheek and then kissed her on the lips, lingering there and enjoying the sensations coursing through his body. Wanting her more than anything else, he forgot himself in her luscious, pouty lips. Reluctantly, he pulled back and sighed as Aimee tugged on his pant leg impatiently.

"Daddy, how come you kissed Miss Twish for so long? You don't kiss Aunt Sylvia that long and you nevew kiss Josie." Aimee asked.

"Well, I'll leave you two to talk about this. I really need to get going. I'll see you later Davis. Thanks again Aimee." Trish said as she turned and chuckled over how Davis was going to explain the kiss to Aimee. It was going to take quite a bit of talking. Aimee wasn't easily fooled and certainly had an inquiring mind.
On Monday morning Trish was sitting at her desk before Melissa came in. She needed to get an early start since she managed to blow-off all the work she'd brought home with her on Friday. When she heard the door open she assumed it was Melissa and stayed seated at her desk. When she looked up she was staring into Davis' handsome face as he walked around where she was sitting. Without a word he bent down and kissed her lips briefly and handed her a single yellow rose.
"Good morning." He said simply as he turned and strode out of her office without another word.
"Morning" Trish called to him once her surprise wore off.
"Good morning Melissa" she heard him say as Melissa replied sleepily "Morning." Melissa was not a morning person.
After Melissa poured her second cup of coffee she felt awake enough for some conversation, so she headed into Trish's office to rehash Saturday night's activities and to get the scoop on the Davis/Trish situation. When they both finished their chronicles, Trish asked.
 "Do you think this you and Larry thing is going anywhere?"

"I don't know. I like him, but time will tell. I'm just going to take it one day at a time and see what happens." Melissa responded. "What about you and Davis?"
"Just like you, one day at a time." But Trish knew she wasn't being completely honest with Melissa. She didn't know what she would do if Davis dumped her, and she knew for sure she wasn't calling it quits. She decided not to think about it right now. She knew she was falling in love, but she didn't want to stop the fall.
"Let's get back to work. I've got a lot of research to do for this carnival fundraiser at the preschool. Have we heard anything back from the elementary school about using their gym?"
"No. Not yet. I'll call them again right now." Melissa replied as she left Trish's office.

Davis sat at his desk, humming contentedly when Larry walked in holding his morning coffee and, without invitation, sat in one of the chairs facing his desk. Larry waited for Davis to look up. When he finally did, Larry exclaimed in a loud whisper.

"You got some noogie this weekend! I can see it in your face! You look so much calmer, serene almost. Here I thought I was going to come in here and rub it in that I got lucky."

"Luck's got nothing to do with it, my man. It's skill, all skill." Davis laughingly informed him.

"Well I guess I don't have to ask you if you had a good time at the party. Shit, I came in here to shoot the bull with you but I guess I already know everything. It's hell to be this good looking *and* smart."

"I know, but I can't figure out how you'd know about such things Larry. You must do a lot of reading." Davis shot back without a pause. Reading had served her well. He shook his head a little and laughed. God she was sweet. *So honest and direct, not to mention sexy as hell.* Better yet, she seemed to have a genuine affection for Aimee, just as Aimee did for her. He had spent the rest of the day trying to explain that kiss to Aimee in terms a four year-old would understand. Every time he thought she understood, she'd pop-up with another question. She was no push-over.

Just as Davis thought that, his interoffice phone rang. Larry got up and just waved goodbye. He looked kind of bummed now because he didn't get to have the anticipated gloating session he had been looking forward to. *Oh well, he'll get over it.*

"Yeah."

"Mr. Sinclair. I have Aimee's pre-school teacher on line one for you."

"Thanks, Terri." A jolt of fear shot through his body.

"Davis Sinclair. May I help you?"

"Yes Mr. Sinclair this is Anna Wells at the Harbor Springs Pre-school. Everything is fine. Aimee is fine. This is just a courtesy call." She said this very quickly to allay any fears he might have had.

"Aimee is such a sweet, happy little girl. I understand you took her to the park yesterday with a *'friend'* of yours and fed the ducks."

"Yessss." Davis said warily. "Aimee told you about it?"

"Oh yes. *ALL* about it, if you get my drift?" Anna Wells hoped he got it, because it was too sticky to explain.

"Ah. I see. This is about the kiss. We had a little bit of confusion we're trying to clear-up on that. You see, Aimee never met her mother and I just started dating again. She's never seen me with anyone but her and other family members. We're working on it." Davis was flustered and that didn't happen often to him.

"She didn't say anything inappropriate, I just wanted to remind you that four year-olds tend to talk about everything they see and think without censure. I'm just trying to head-off a potentially embarrassing situation for you. This is a small town and word gets around fast among the mothers of the children." Anna was trying to be as tactful as possible, and Davis appreciated it.

"Thank you. I understand what you're saying and I'm grateful that you took the time to let me know Ms. Wells. I assure you I'll do everything I can to clear-up this little matter. Was that all you needed Ms. Wells?"

"Yes that's it. Thank you, Mr. Sinclair. Goodbye." Anna let out a long breath as she hung-up the phone. That went better than she thought it would. She hated having to make those kinds of calls.

Chapter 12

Things between Trish and Davis continued to escalate as the weeks went by. They saw each other as often as possible, making love whenever and wherever they could. Usually going out to the movies and to Moody's as their schedules permitted.

Every morning Davis stopped at Trish's office for what was now their traditional good morning kiss, sometimes a little more groping than kissing took place. That was fine with Trish, and she had never heard Davis complain either, they fit well together on every level. Trish had also come to love Aimee too. She was such a delight to be around. She had a sweet nature about her, innocent, loving people, animals, and even little babies. Davis had invited Trish to go trick-or-treating with them. Aimee looked so adorable in her little lady bug costume, her antenna jiggling as she skipped happily down the sidewalk of Davis' neighborhood. She held her plastic pumpkin bucket tightly in both hands, afraid she would spill her priceless treasure. She never had to be told to say thank you or please. She didn't even complain when she got pennies or the occasional apple for her treat.

Trish felt a little sorry for Davis sometimes. It wasn't easy being involved with someone who worked almost every weekend, but they had worked out a system where he would meet her at her apartment after whatever event she had worked and they would finish the evening together. Eventually Trish had even given him a key to her apartment. Sometimes Davis would go to her apartment early and set a romantic atmosphere by placing lit candles around the room and having a snack prepared, just a little something to keep their strength up in between lovemaking sessions. Alright, so now she was starting to understand a little bit of the romance thing people always talked about. Trish had never been so happy. She never realized this kind of happiness even existed, let alone that it would happen to her.

The carnival Trish organized for the pre-school was a huge success. The crowds were just beginning to thin out when Trish heard Aimee screech in delight.

"Miss Twish! Look, I won a teddy beaw at the bean bag toss game!" Her little cheeks were flushed with excitement as she ran up to Trish. Josie, the nanny, trailed sluggishly behind Aimee with another woman who looked remarkably like Josie, probably her sister. Trish had met Josie a few times now and liked her a lot. Her story was one of tragedy and triumph, having raised three boys of her own when her husband died suddenly. She struggled financially but refused to give up and decided to become a nanny to other people who needed her. She was short, about five one ,with graying brown hair and a medium build, probably near fifty years old Trish guessed, but had the energy of someone half her age. She was very good with Aimee but today she looked very pale, almost green actually.

"Wow! You must be so proud!" Trish said excitedly to Aimee. She looked at Josie with concern.

"Are you alright Josie, you don't look like you're feeling very well."

"Maybe just a bit of the flu, but I couldn't disappoint Aimee and not bring her to the carnival. Trish, this is my sister, Helen. Helen this is Trish Haywood, she's a friend of Mr. Sinclair's." Josie swayed a little and steadied herself on Helen's arm.

Trish was alarmed and gave Helen a meaningful look of concern.

"You know Josie we're almost done with the carnival here and I think maybe Helen needs to take you to a doctor. How about if I call Mr. Sinclair and let him know I'll keep Aimee with me until he's available. Then you can get some rest and let Helen take care of you. You're always taking care of other people, now I think it's your turn to be taken care of."

"Oh, I don't know how Mr. Sinclair would feel about that. I don't want him to get angry."

"Let's call him right now and find out." Trish dialed Davis' office. She knew he had a deposition that was going to take most of the day so she dialed the office phone instead of his cell phone. Trish told Terri she needed to speak to Davis and that, although not an emergency, it was urgent. A few minutes later Davis came on the phone and Trish explained the situation.

"I just don't think it's a good idea for Josie to take care of Aimee today. Since I dialed your office she's thrown-up twice. I really think it's better if Aimee and I just hang out together this afternoon. You can pick her up when you're done at the office. Helen will take care of Josie."

"I can't tell you how much I appreciate you doing this Trish. You're a lifesaver."

"Hey, I love the kid and we'll have a lot of fun together. I'm really looking forward to our girls day out."

"Okay. I'll let you get back to work and I'll see you later." Trish hung up the phone. Trish turned her attention back to Josie and Helen. Helen had gotten Aimee's booster seat for Trish from Josie's car and carefully led Josie away.

Trish and Aimee ended-up having a wonderful afternoon together. They went to the Harbor Springs Pet Stop and looked at all the animals for sale. They cooed to and stroked all the animals they could. Aimee enjoyed looking at all the different types of fish they had on display and she got to see some lizards and snakes, but those were looked at from a distance. They were a little too slimy to get close to, in their opinion. The ferrets were actively playing with each other and Aimee giggled endlessly at their antics. When they were leaving the parking lot, Trish noticed they were having a pet adoption event in the parking lot. When she and Aimee went inside the tent, Trish looked up into the face of the most adorable kitten she had ever seen. It stared at her with its big, round green eyes and a pushed-in nose on its monkey face. It had long, solid grey fur that was in total disarray. Trish fell head over heels in love with him and knew he was the cat for her. Without hesitation Trish approached the pet adoption people and told her she wanted to adopt him. As Trish finished the endless paperwork required for the adoption the woman conducting the event looked down at Aimee.

"You're a lucky little girl to be getting such a sweet little kitty. You know you have to be gentle with him, right?"

Aimee's eyes went wide and Trish knew by her expression that she thought the kitten was for her. Trish had to think fast.

"You know Aimee that the kitty has to live all the time at my house, but we can share him. Do you think you could help me name him?" Trish tried to distract her and clarify her intent at the same time.

"Okay. But I can come to yow house and visit him, wight?" Aimee asked sweetly as the disappointment showed on her little face.

"Absolutely! Now we need to go back into the pet store and get some supplies for him before we take him to my house. Would you mind being in charge of picking out his toys?" Her face brightened considerably and she happily nodded her head in agreement as she took Trish's hand and led her back into the store. They bought so much stuff Trish was sure the stock boys would need a week to restock the shelves. They loaded the little kitten into his new carrier and finally left, her car considerably more crowded than when they'd arrived. Trish let the kitten sit in the back seat with Aimee as Trish drove through Speedy Burger and got Aimee the healthful kiddie meal. She didn't want to take any chances and fill her little tummy with junk food, so she ordered as healthfully as possible at a drive-through joint.

When they got to her apartment Aimee helped Trish set-up all the kitty paraphernalia to get no name settled in. Aimee lifted the heavy food bag, grunting with the effort, but fiercely determined to get the bag to the kitchen. Aimee had already placed the food and water bowls on the special kitty placemat she had helped pick out. Aimee decided that Trish's bedroom was the best place for the litter box, reasoning out that he could have more privacy as he did his number one and number two. They placed the kitty gym and his fluffy bed in the corner of the living room near the bookshelves. Aimee opened all the packages of toys and put them inside the basket they had bought to store them in. Aimee played with the kitten while Trish cleaned-up the trash. She squealed in delight as the kitten chased the feather attached to the end of the stick that she swished in the air. Trish changed into sweats and made herself a cup of coffee while Aimee played. When she went back into the living room both the kitten and Aimee were sound asleep on the floor, curled into each other. The kitten purred loudly in his sleep as Aimee sighed in her own little dream world. Trish covered Aimee with a throw from the back of the couch and turned on the television quietly while she drank her coffee and relaxed. Soon she too was sound asleep.

When Davis let himself into Trish's apartment he saw the two of them and was sure his heart would burst out of his chest. The two people he loved most in the world. Sound asleep without a care in the world. He had to blink back the tears of joy that stung his eyes. He wanted to come home to this scene every night. He sat in the chair across from Trish and let the emotions sweep over him.

Trish opened her eyes and was surprised to see Davis sitting across from her.
"Oh, Davis, I didn't hear you come in." She crawled off the couch toward him.
"I guess we kind of zonked out. How long have you been here?"
Davis reached up and pulled Trish onto his lap and enveloped her in his arms as he kissed her over and over without saying a word. Trish laid her head on his shoulder and cuddled. She kissed his neck and continued to kiss her way down his jaw line until she reached his lips. She kissed him once, lovingly, then laid her head back onto his shoulder. They sat there without speaking, just holding each other, until Aimee woke up.
 When Aimee realized where Trish and Davis were she got up and crawled into Davis' lap across from Trish. Davis thought his legs would fall off as his muscles complained and then fell asleep, but he just didn't care. He had everything in the world he needed in his lap right now.
 "Daddy, guess what? Twish got me a kitty cat, a weal live one and evewything! Look he's sleeping on the floow ovew thewe." She pointed with her pudgy little finger in the direction of the sleeping kitten. Davis glanced to the floor and glared at Trish.
 "Wow. That is so..." all he could think of were negatives.
"Aimee we need to explain the rules about the kitty to your daddy so he understands." Trish looked into Davis' eyes as she spoke.
 "The kitty is going to live here at my house where Aimee can visit him anytime she wants, right Aimee?" Aimee nodded her head in agreement. Relief swept over Davis' face, although he was still just a little put-out over the whole situation.
"And you can't squeeze him and you have to hold him with two hands." Aimee added with a stern look of warning directed at Davis. Aimee was taking her parenting responsibilities *very* seriously.

"Now all we need is a name for him." Trish added. They ordered pizza for dinner and ate together as they discussed name possibilities. Various names were batted around Gaston, Beast, Fred, Gargoyle, Henry, Furry, Fuzzy, but in the end everyone finally agreed on Romeo. Aimee entertained them with her stories about the carnival and of course their adventures at the pet store. With dinner over they all sat on the living room floor and played with Romeo until he was tired out. Aimee sat at the kitchen table and drew a picture of Romeo for Trish. Trish had insisted that Aimee sign the picture like a *real* artist. Trish took Aimee's colored picture, put it in a frame, and hung it on the wall right over Romeo's bed. Aimee was so proud that Trish had hung her picture in the living room where everyone could see it. When Aimee started to rub her eyes it signaled Davis it was time to go. Of course that involved the raspberries/kissing routine they had done in the park several weeks ago. Trish thought it was sweet. When they were gone she collapsed onto the couch and didn't move the rest of the night. *Having a kid was tiring.* Trish drifted off to sleep. Romeo ignored his cushy bed and instead laid down with Trish on the couch, purring contentedly as he slept.

Chapter 13

With the holidays quickly approaching Trish's business was running wild. Both Trish and Melissa were working killer hours and seven days a week. There were times when Trish had to rely on Melissa to run some events so she could attend a second event on the same night. As an incentive for Melissa, Trish paid her triple time if she had to attend an event on a weekend. Trish knew that eventually she would have to give-up attending events herself and hire more help, but frankly she was a control freak when it came to her business and reputation. If she planned it, or her company rather, she was responsible for its success and she took any failure of things to run smoothly as a personal failure. With the holiday parties in full swing, Trish had a policy of confirming each contractor three times per event. Better safe than sorry. Most nights Trish fell into bed well after midnight and was up and at the office again by eight the next morning. Davis had given Trish a good idea, although he had said it jokingly, to put a daybed in her office so she wouldn't have to waste time commuting back and forth to work. Once Trish thought about it she decided it was actually a very good idea and ordered one online the next day.

Trish and Melissa found themselves continually apologizing to Larry and Davis for making them go stag to their own functions, functions that everyone else went to as couples. The four of them even joked that Larry and Davis were dating. Davis thought Trish should get a Do Not Disturb sign for her office door, that way they could make good use of the daybed in Trish's office. Although using the day bed was a good idea, Trish thought a sign would be tacky. A lock on the door would work much better. To help out, Larry and Davis often got take-out for dinner and the four of them would eat together in Trish's conference room. Trish still adored Davis and felt her heart tug each time she laid eyes on him. Melissa and Larry seemed to be really hitting it off as well, although Melissa had never admitted to Trish she was in love, she knew her friend well enough to know she only had eyes for Larry.

Davis was fighting his own battles with the holiday parties lining up like soldiers on his calendar. If he didn't absolutely have to attend he didn't. He was never really the partying type anyway, he'd rather spend the night with Aimee or Trish than hang around bullshitting with some of the arrogant social types his aunt and uncle insisted he socialize with. Even though Aunt Sylvia was well aware Davis was in a 'committed' relationship, she still continually insisted on trying to fix him up with more socially acceptable dates. Uncle Jake just ignored Aunt Sylvia's attempts at matchmaking with a shrug that implied his typical male surrender to all of Aunt Sylvia's escapades. When it came to dealing with Aunt Sylvia Davis was on his own. Sylvia was relentless in her pursuit to find him an 'acceptable' wife and mother for Aimee.

Who in their right mind chose to get married between Thanksgiving and New Years. Isn't it hectic enough for everyone without the added burden of attending a wedding, not to mention the financial impact on their already strained budget's. To top everything off, this wedding was running like the wedding from hell. Guests would never know by looking that Trish was running like a chicken with her head cut-off, fixing one disaster after another. Oven's broke, flower orders were wrong, cake was late arriving, you name it and it went wrong. As Trish was rushing around a corner she looked-up and to her surprise saw Davis standing in the hallway outside the restrooms wearing a tuxedo and holding a drink in his hand.

"Davis, I didn't know you were invited to this wedding tonight."

"Trish, um, I, um, you're organizing this wedding?" His face showed complete shock as the color drained from it.

"I didn't realize you knew the Cole's or the McNeal's. Where do you know them from?"

Trish began to get a sinking feeling in the pit of her stomach. The bile rose in her throat as a beautiful blonde walked-up to Davis and locked her arm around his in a gesture of possession. She was tall, with legs up to her eyes and she wore a cocktail dress that showed off those legs to an almost indecent degree. Slim and sexy, with long blonde hair styled in the latest fashion, enhanced her aristocratic features. Long nails were painted a bright holiday red to bring attention to her slim fingers. Trish's heart sank as the realization of what she was seeing sank into her mind. Never had she ever expected Davis to cheat on her. She had been so sure of him. Trish literally felt her heart break in half. Sadness. Anger. Hurt. Indignation. All of them flashing through her at mind and heart at lightening speed. She didn't know what to do. She was frozen in place as her mind screamed. *RUN!* She told herself to think, to do something, anything, to escape the pain coursing through her very soul. He was her heart, her love, and he had betrayed her. The blonde looked totally bored with the whole situation.

"Davis, why are you hanging out with the hired help? Is there a problem?" She smiled a bitchy, superior smile as she hugged his arm closer. "You know, we really should get back to Sylvia and Jake. We don't want people to start speculating that we've gone off and eloped already."

Davis tried to ignore her. He wanted to explain that this was all a mistake. He was only doing a favor for Aunt Sylvia by escorting, what's her name? Sheila. Right. Sheila, to this wedding. Instead he found himself introducing them to each other.

"Trish, I'd like you to meet Sheila Cole. Sheila Cole, this is Trish Haywood." They nodded to each other like fierce competitors. His heart was going to beat out of his chest as his face reddened in embarrassment. He couldn't grasp the right words to make a complete sentence, as he stared at Trish. After a few moments Davis cleared his throat and instead of introducing them he blurted out the first thing that came to his mind.

"Trish, this isn't what it looks like. Well it is, but it isn't what you think." he stuttered.

"You have no idea what I'm thinking Davis." Trish said coldly.

"Please, I can explain. It's really all very innocent."

"Okay. Shoot. I'm listening." Trish crossed her arms over her chest.

"Well, Sheila here needed an escort tonight so Aunt Sylvia called and asked me if I would help her out. I didn't have any plans so I agreed."

Sheila chose this moment to add her two cents into the conversation.

"Sylvia told me you were looking for a wife and mother for your daughter. She said you weren't involved with anyone and because you were new in town you hadn't had a chance to meet any or the right people. Really Davis, I'm shocked you would even consider dating the hired help. You really need to raise your standards."

"Well that certainly clears things up for me. You're right Sheila. I guess it was my mistake. Please, by all means enjoy your evening." By the time Trish finished speaking tears were streaming down her face. She ran out into the night. Blinded by her tears, she just walked for hours.

She had no idea where she was going or what she was doing, all she knew was that she had to get out of there. Find somewhere where it didn't hurt so much. The pain took her breath away as she sat on the steps of a building. She didn't know exactly where she was and didn't care. She sat and sobbed until the tears had run their course. The pain she felt washed over her in enormous waves, over and over again. No matter where she went the pain followed her. She felt so betrayed, she never, ever thought Davis would do this to her. Trish searched her memory, trying to see if she had missed any of what she thought were the classic signs of infidelity. Was she really that blind and naïve? Apparently the answer was yes.

Trish knew she didn't want to go home. Too painful. Too many memories. What used to be happy memories were now just lies. She headed toward her office realizing her daybed was going to come in very handy tonight.

How could she have been so stupid? She felt like a fool. She vowed to herself that she would never put herself in this position again. *The nun's had been right after all.* If you sequestered yourself you never had to deal with the pain and heartache in life. Why had it taken her so long to see their point of view? With that thought Trish drifted off to sleep. Sometime later, she had no idea how much later, she heard a muffled voice in the outer office. She recognized the voice as Melissa's but she couldn't make out what was being said. She really didn't care. All she wanted right now was to be left alone. She was numb and as long as she stayed that way she didn't have to feel the pain. Knowing there was no way Melissa would just go away she opened her office door.

"Melissa what are you doing here?" She said it with no feeling or inflection in her voice. Flat. Completely devoid of all emotion. Trish's face was swollen from all the crying she had done, lord knows Melissa had been there before herself.

"Davis called me. He was worried about you. He told me what happened. I'm so sorry Trish. I know you love him. He said he stayed at your apartment all night waiting for you and that you never showed-up. He was frantic with worry and asked me to come and see if you were here. That was him I was talking to on the phone just now."

"Well now you can tell him you found me. I'm sure I'll survive, others have and so can I. I just wish he could have been honest with me. If he wanted to see other people he should have told me. But live and learn, isn't that the saying? Now I've learned." Trish took a deep breath to steady her nerves and then flatly asked Melissa for help.

"Okay." Melissa agreed immediately.

"Could you please go to my apartment and wait for the locksmith to change my locks, and then bring the new keys back. I don't want to talk to anyone right now." Trish turned and walked back into her office, locking the door behind her.

Melissa's heart sank as she heard the click of the lock on Trish's office door. This was a lot worse than she thought it would be. She could understand anger, rage, tears all the normal emotions associated with the hurt that love sometimes brought, but the icy coldness in Trish's eyes terrified her. Cold detachment. As if her blood had been replaced with ice.

Melissa had been right to worry. For several weeks now Trish had barely spoken. She answered her questions, returned and made phone calls, even smiled. But the smiles were fake, plastic, pasted on for the benefit of the clients, as soon as their backs were turned she went back to the same stoic face that was devoid of all emotion. Like a walking zombie. She was losing weight but Melissa couldn't get her to eat. The dark circles under her eyes were covered with make-up daily. Quite a few times Melissa had walked into Trish's office to find her staring off into space, absorbed in her own thoughts. Melissa felt so helpless, unable to console her friend, and cried herself some days at the loss of her friend.

Davis had tried to patch things up with Trish but she wouldn't have anything to do with him. He'd seen her through the glass of her office door, but he knew she wasn't really there. She was just going through the motions necessary to get through her day. Melissa had even come to him, crying and fearful for her friend, but there was nothing anyone could do. Trish wouldn't let anyone in and it was his fault. He had let his Aunt Sylvia play on his emotions and interfere in his life because he was insecure enough from his first marriage to not trust himself completely when it came to judging Trish's character. His first wife had been a money hungry whore who had taken Davis for everything he had, except Aimee. That was where he had drawn the line. Aunt Sylvia had pointed out that since he had a 'history' of going out with, and marrying, unsuitable women, maybe he should let her help him find someone suitable. All this done under the guise of love. Eventually he finally fell for it. What an ass he'd been. Now he had lost the first women he had ever felt completely compatible with, his soul mate, his heart. He could try to make excuses for himself. Blame other people, even Aunt Sylvia, but bottom line was he screwed-up by not having enough faith in himself or Trish.

Chapter 14

As the holidays came and went things at the office began to calm down some. Not many people got married in January and February. Trish's main focus was on the town's Winter Frost Festival. It was by far the largest event Trish and Melissa had ever handled and was held in the city's park. They had to deal with committee, sub-committee, charities, city workers and the mayor in order to coordinate all the activities. The event was to take place in the middle of February. Valentine's Day. It would be a one day event that would have every winter activity anyone could think of. Each charity was assigned one event to run, and in turn got to keep the profits from that event. The city was sponsoring the free events such as ice skating, sledding, warming stations, they were even kicking-off the event with a polar bear swim at noon. Sponsors were hosting the games such as snowshoe races and snowman building contests and some other nonprofit events like a sled dog racing exhibition and ice sculpting demonstrations. Some guy with a bulldozer even volunteered to build a bunny hill for kids to try skiing on. One thing in their favor was that the community had embraced the idea and volunteers poured in to help. Trish and Melissa kept a planning board in Trish's office just to keep everything straight. Food vendors and a fireworks expert were the responsibility of Celebrations along with the coordination of the event. Trish had the city string all the trees and poles along the walkway in the park with white Christmas lights. The effect of the lights at night was absolutely, breathtakingly beautiful. The finale of the night would be the fireworks display over the frozen pond in the center of the park. A combination of three bands would be playing throughout the day in the gazebo, with a sing-along scheduled for seven at night. Every song sang had to have something to do with cold, winter, snow or anything one associated with winter activities. A children's sing-along was scheduled for six o'clock with special characters in costume circulating throughout the crowd as they passed out candy. Trish prayed for snow, which was a first for her, and hoped it melted the day after the festival. If the weather didn't cooperate, Trish had lined-up a few snow-making machines to ensure a successful event. All and all this kept Trish's mind occupied and each night she went home, exhausted, to Romeo, who faithfully kept her company.

For the first time since opening Celebrations It felt like a job to Trish. In the past she enjoyed the planning and organization that was required to pull-off a function, now it was a burden she was anxious to be rid of. Trish had decided to make an appointment with Jake Sullivan after the festival was over to talk to him about turning the running of the company over to Melissa. Jake Sullivan was the only person that knew about Trish's past. He had been her grandfather's friend and oversaw the family fortune that Trish had inherited when she turned twenty one. At Jake's insistence Trish had kept the fact that she was a rich heiress to herself. For security purposes, he had explained and Trish had honored his request without questions. If not for Jake she could have never started her own company seven years ago. He was the closest thing to a father she had ever known.

Larry came rushing into Celebrations like his ass was on fire, visibly shaken. All he said to Melissa was, "I need to talk to both of you right now, Trish is here isn't she?"

"Yeah. What's wrong Larry you're scaring me here?" Melissa rose slowly from her chair as Trish came rushing out of her office.

Larry blurted out.

"Jake Sullivan is in a hospital in London and Davis just took off for the airport to join Sylvia there. They don't know what's wrong with him, just that he collapsed in his hotel room last night." All the color had drained out of Larry's face as he plopped down into one of the chairs in the reception area.

"Oh my god that's awful. Jake was such a help to me when I first came here. Davis must be frantic with worry. Larry, do you have Davis' contact information, I need to talk to him." Trish asked.

Both Melissa and Larry stared at her in amazement. "Yeah. I mean, I can get it."

"Good. I need you to go get it right now, and I want both of you to be in my office when I call."

Chapter 15

When they were all seated around Trish's desk Melissa dialed Davis' phone number for her. Trish knew he was still in transit but she needed to get this over with as soon as possible. She had learned that Davis had chartered a private plane to take him to London.

When Davis' phone rang he jumped and looked at the display. *Celebrations? Now what?* He answered his phone with gruffly, not sure how much more bad news he could take. He was ready to fracture.

"Davis Sinclair." He had expected to be talking to Melissa so when Trish's voice sounded his heart gave a wild leap of anticipation.

"Hi, Davis. It's Trish. I know this is a bad time for you, but I have to talk to you. Just to let you know, Melissa and Larry are here with me and you're on speaker phone right now."

"Are you all right?" he asked simply. That made Trish's heart ache even more. It touched her that he had concern for her when he must be going crazy over his uncle.

"Yes I'm fine. It's you and your Uncle Jake that I'm worried about." *Aunt Sylvia could burn in hell.* She had figured-out that Sylvia had manipulated the whole date Davis had gone on and, having dealt with her in the past, she was aware of how 'persuasive' Sylvia could be. It didn't excuse Davis from guilt but it explained some of the pressure he was under to find a 'suitable' mate.

"Davis I want to offer you my full support for whatever your uncle may need. I owe a great deal to Jake. He was the only person I knew when I first moved here seven years ago. He helped me establish Celebrations and taught me how to run it. He also handles all my financial affairs for me. I'm the sole heir to the Haywood Lumber fortune, so if Jake needs anything to insure his health or comfort please don't hesitate to call me. If you can't reach me tell Melissa or Larry and they'll find me for

73

you. Davis, you don't have to ask first either, use my name to insure payment for anything you feel he needs."

When Trish told them that she's a heiress, Melissa and Larry's jaws dropped in unison. Never would they have guessed that Trish came from money. Tons of money. More money than anyone could ever spend on three lifetimes.

"Davis, are you still there?" Trish asked.

"Yeah. Um, that's really generous of you Trish. I'm sure my uncle will appreciate your help and concern." Still in disbelief he struggled to speak.

"Trish, why didn't you tell me any of this before?"

"I wanted to, but your uncle convinced me that it would be better if we kept it to ourselves for safety reasons. I'm taking a chance in letting you three know, I'm sure your uncle will yell at me as soon as he can, and I'm trusting all of you to keep my secret for me. I just don't want anything bad to happen to Jake, he's my oldest friend and the closest thing to a father I've ever known." Trish let out a long breath and sat back in her chair.

"Trish, you have a heart of gold and I'm an idiot. I appreciate you giving me another chance at showing you I can be trusted. I won't let you down. I promise. Please let me tell you again how sorry I am that I hurt you. I'll never forgive myself for messing-up the best thing that ever happened to me, and that would be you Trish. I miss you and I have no one to blame but myself." Davis' heart broke as he heard the sadness in Trish's voice. The sadness he caused. He didn't want to hang-up the phone so he continued to talk about anything that popped into his head.

"How's Romeo? Has he gotten a lot bigger? He's still all Aimee talks about."

"Romeo's doing great. He really hasn't grown that much, apparently his breed of cat stays close to kitten size, so he's still just as adorable. Tell Aimee she's welcome to come and visit anytime she likes, and that I miss her."

"Well Davis I'll let you go now, I'm sure you have a lot to take care of. Call me if you need anything?" Trish quickly hung-up the phone and looked at Melissa and Larry.

"So now you both know everything. If Davis, Sylvia, or Jake call, please find me immediately. If you can't find me, authorize whatever it is on my behalf. I know I can trust you both to not say anything to anyone about my family connections."

Both Melissa and Larry nodded their heads in agreement and left the office together.

Chapter 16

Plans for the festival continued on schedule over the next couple of days. There had been good news on Jake, apparently he had a hiatal hernia but the symptoms mimic those of a heart attack. Jake, Davis and Sylvia were all back in the United States and, just to be sure, Jake was going to a doctor here for a second opinion. As Trish was walking through the lobby of her office building, she saw the same man that she had seen the last two days standing in front of the florist. She remembered him because he looked out of place among all the other office workers. His hair was red and unkempt with long, bushy muttonchops and coke bottle glasses with black plastic frames. He hadn't changed his clothes since the first day she'd seen him which was gross in itself. He wore dirty jeans, a grey t-shirt under a drab olive green hoodie that zipped up the front. His mannerisms were nervous and jerky as his eyes darted around the lobby. Trish shuttered as she stepped onto the elevator where Davis just happened to be standing.

She looked up into his eyes as her heart did a high dive off the jumping board of a pool. Trish just nodded her head as a hello to Davis.

"Are you all right, I saw you shudder and that was even before you saw me." He hoped she would get the intended humor.

"Yeah, um, that guy in the green hoodie just gives me the creeps. He's here every day now. I'm just paranoid, I'm sure."

Davis looked at him as the doors slid shut on the elevator. "You know he does look out of place for an office building. I'll talk to the security guard and ask him to keep an eye out for him."

"Oh, really, you don't have to do that. I'll call him myself. I don't want to put you to any trouble." She said nervously.

"Trish, you've never been any trouble to me. Please let me do this for you." Trish thought about it for a second and then relented.

"Okay." was all she was able to get out before the elevator doors opened onto their floor. Trish entered her office and didn't give the incident another thought as her mind shifted back to the festival once more. Today Trish was going to go stalking businesses for raffle prizes. After being in the business so long, Trish had learned to hate making phone calls for an entire day, but some days that was exactly what was needed. As was customary for Harbor Springs, the response was overwhelmingly generous. Grand Prize was going to be a cruise for four on a Disney cruise ship. Second prize was a spa weekend in Arizona. Third prize a $1000.00 gift card to the local Piggly Wiggly supermarket. With prizes like these they were going to have to start selling tickets two weeks before the festival outside all the local stores. Usually the best group at raising funds were, surprisingly, the pre-school's students and kindergarten classes at the local elementary school. Who could resist the toothless grin of a child as they asked, politely of course, if you wanted to buy a 'waffle twicket'. It worked every time, even on people who didn't live in the town. Parents of course would help out by bringing the tickets to work and sell them to anyone who passed their desk. There would be a special prize for the top salesperson in each class of the elementary and middle school as an incentive. *Kids loved that kind of stuff.* She added yet more information to the planning board in her office. Trish stood in front of the planning board and rubbed the back of her neck as she checked it over for accuracy or to see if she had missed anything. She felt a pair of strong, warm hands gently push hers aside as they took over the kneading of her tense muscles. She looked behind her to see Davis standing there looking at the board over her head as he massaged her neck. *God he was good at this.* A small moan of pleasure escaped her lips before she could suppress it.

"You're working too hard, your neck is one big knot." He bent down to talk into her ear. His hot breath sending shivers down her neck.

"It's a big job putting all of this together. What brings you to our humble office?" Trish was melting into a liquid pool of mush at his touch. She tried to move away so she could face him but he stopped her and turned her back toward the board, resuming the massage.

"I talked to the security people about that guy in the lobby this morning and they want me to notify them the minute we see him again. They claim they've already talked to him a couple of times but he keeps coming back. Since he's not breaking the law, they can't force him to leave the premises but they can stand there and stare him down until he leaves the building. I told them I'd be the contact person on this, so let me know and then I'll let them know if you see him again."

"Okay, thanks for handling that for me, I was on the phone so much today I thought someone was going to have to surgically remove it from my ear."

"One other thing, Aimee was wondering if she could come over on Sunday and see Romeo. I told her you were really busy right now but that I'd ask anyway." It was shameless the way he was using Aimee as an excuse to see Trish but he was desperate.

"Um, actually, that would be really great. What time were you thinking?" Trish surprised herself at how excited she felt at the thought of seeing both Davis and Aimee. She had to admit she missed them. Her resolve to stay aloof was falling by the wayside as he continued to massage her shoulders.

"How's eleven sound?"

"Yeah, that sounds great. I'll make sure Romeo gets all his beauty sleep.

"Great! She'll be so excited."

Trish looked up just as Melissa was giving Davis the thumbs-up sign.

When Davis was gone Trish called Melissa into her office in a sing-song tone.

"Are you plotting with Davis behind my back? Trying to arrange a get together between the two of us?"

"Who, me? Would I do something like that to you?" She batted her eyelashes demurely at Trish.

"Of course you would."

"I'd like to take credit for it, I really would, but not this time. Although, if I were you I wouldn't entirely rule out the possibility in the future." Melissa giggled.

"Thanks for the warning. Also, have you noticed this kind of grungy red headed guy hanging around the lobby, a real jittery type?"

"Ewwwe, you mean that guy? He gives me the creeps."

"That's the guy. If you see him again you need to let Davis know. He got a look at him this morning and he contacted security about it. They want to know if we see him again. Just to be safe, don't get into the elevator with him, something about him really freaks me out."

"You got it."

"Great. I thought we could go over the board before we leave." Trish said.

"No. Not the board! Anything but the board! I don't have anything to add to it."

"Well I added our raffle prizes and a few other things. Nothing that can't wait until Monday. Let's get the hell out of here. I've had enough for today."

Chapter 17

Sunday came quickly as Trish put the final touches on the tray of treats she was preparing for the tea party she had planned for Aimee and Davis' visit. Aimee would love it, Davis would tolerate it for Aimee. Trish set the kitchen table with frilly, girly, girl linen which matched with coordinating plates, tea pot and matching cups with saucer. Trish had one platter filled with tea sandwiches of all varieties, crusts removed of course, and cut into triangles. The second platter was filled with pastries of all kinds. Both platters had been lined with lace doilies. She planned on making Earl Grey tea in the teapot but had bought juice boxes, beer and pop just in case Aimee didn't like tea. Trish had even thought to buy sugar cubes and put them in the matching sugar bowl with tongs. Aimee would like the tong idea.

Trish was nervous. She jumped at the knock on the door. Trish opened the door to see Aimee with a bouquet of wildflowers and Davis standing behind her, smiling broadly.

"Miss Twish we gotted you these flowews. Whewe is Womeo?" Aimee

Asked anxiously.

"Thank you Aimee they're beautiful. Did you pick them out yourself?"

"Yep. Daddy had to weach them but I pointed to them fow him." Trish gushed over them a few minutes more before putting them in water. She made a point of putting them in the center of the table, gushing genuinely at the sweet thought. Davis took their coats and laid them on the bed in Trish's room. By the time he came out Aimee was already on the floor playing with Romeo. Trish put the flowers on the table as a centerpiece and turned to see Davis watching Aimee play as she giggled and danced as Romeo chased the feather she was waving around for him.

"Davis can I get you something to drink, I have pretty much anything you want, although don't ask for tea, we're having a tea party a little later." Trish laughed at the expression on Davis' face when she mentioned the tea party.

"Whatever you're having will be fine."

"Well, do you think Romeo has grown much since you last saw him?" Trish asked as she poured their pop into glasses.

"No, not really. How old is he now?"

"Um. About seven months old I think."

Aimee called Davis from the living room

"Watch me daddy. Watch me play with Wormeo."

"Okay, I'm coming right now."

Trish and Davis both went into the living room to watch Romeo's antics. Twice he climbed the drapes and Aimee insisted Davis rescue him both times. One thing was for sure, both Aimee and Romeo were going to sleep good tonight. Out of the blue Aimee turned to Trish and asked

"Awe you still mad at daddy? He said he did a weally, weally bad thing and you awe mad at him. It's not good to stay mad, Josie told me that."

Davis put his hands over his face and shook his head, moaning the whole time. When he looked up Aimee was on Trish's lap with her hands on Trish's cheeks, their foreheads touching and Aimee looking intently into Trish's eyes.

"Let me ask you a question. If I forgive your daddy do you promise to come and visit Romeo more often?" Aimee nodded her head yes vigorously.

"Okay, then I forgive daddy." Trish answered with a smile. "I also planned a surprise for you today. Do you think you would like to have a tea party with daddy and me?"

"A weal live tea pawty? Yeah!" The idea was a success.

"Let's go. It's all set-up in the kitchen." Aimee took both Trish and Davis' hands and led the way into the kitchen. Aimee insisted they all follow proper etiquette, according to Aimee's rules. Trish had been right, Aimee loved the tongs. They both had to have at least five sugar cubes in their tea as Trish and Davis pretended to drink the tea. When they were done eating Aimee went into the living room while Davis and Trish cleaned-up.

"I noticed you don't have anymore books on your bookshelves, how come?"

"Those were just fairy tales. Romance isn't real. I guess I just outgrew them." Trish answered honestly. "I donated them to the library."

It took Davis a few minutes to work up the courage to ask the burning question.

"Have you really forgiven me? I need to let you know I *did not* coach her at all, she did all that on her own."

"Yes, I've really forgiven you. Life's too short to hold a grudge. I realized that when Jake was sick." Davis took Trish into his arms and just held her for a few minutes before he kissed her on the lips.

"Thank you. I promise I will never disappoint you again. God, I've missed you so much." He kissed her again, embracing her while she rested her head on his shoulder. Her arms tightened around his waist.

"Davis, that doesn't mean we can go back to the way things were. I'm not the same person I was before, but I do value your friendship and Aimee's. I hope you understand it's not to punish you. I don't want to be with anyone ever again. I made mistakes too, and one of those mistakes was to give in to my body without using my head. I won't make the same mistake twice otherwise this whole situation we went through was for nothing. Do you understand?"

"Yes I understand but I don't like it. I'm not going to lie to you. Every time I see you I want you back, romantically as well as friendship. So you'll forgive me if I still hold out hope that our friendship will turn into something more." Davis wasn't going to give in. He couldn't accept just friendship but he was a very patient man, he could wait. At least this was a start. A rush of relief and love coursed through his body. He wouldn't let the opportunity slip through his fingers again no matter what Aunt Sylvia said or did.

"That's up to you. I can't be responsible for your actions, only my own. If you meet someone who interests you, you're free to explore that relationship. Clearly I wasn't the one to do that for you but I sincerely hope you find who you're looking for. I want you to be happy and until you find that special someone I'd be proud to be you friend. That's all I can offer."

"I'll take it." *For now.*

"Good. You know suddenly it's very quiet in there." She pointed toward the living room. When they got to the living room they saw Aimee sitting on the floor with her legs crossed and Romeo curled-up in a ball on her lap, purring happily while he slept. Aimee put a finger to her lips to keep Trish and Davis quiet and whispered, "He's sleeping. Don't wake him up."

Davis gave her the okay sign and Trish nodded her head. Trish went into the kitchen and grabbed her camera, taking pictures of Aimee and Romeo, then had Davis join in for more pictures. Romeo never woke-up. When Aimee showed signs of tiredness Davis packed her into her coat and took her home. It had been a good day for Trish, one of the best in a long time.

She felt good about the talk she had with Davis. Thank goodness for Aimee. She was the glue that held Davis and Trish until they were able to work things out for themselves. Trish turned on the television and laid on the couch, soon she too was fast asleep.

As the festival got closer Melissa and Trish kicked it into high gear. Trish kept in touch with all the various committee members and now had weekly meetings scheduled for all the committee chairmen. There had been a few additions to the schedule as they added dog sled rides for the children around the perimeter of the pond and a mirror maze. They had so many activities scheduled Trish was sure the park would explode, but then that was the fun of it all. Trish decided they would do a huge publicity blitz the week before. They also decided to print-up an event schedule and have them available throughout the park along with putting one in their print ads. Raffle tickets were printed and ready for sale, which was starting this weekend. One thing Trish decided to do on her own was hire a professional photographer to capture the event on film. She didn't want pictures of the organizers as much as live action shots of the events, something for everyone's memories.

When she took the time off she intended to, she would make scrapbooks for some of the organizations that benefited from the event. For now Trish was keeping the whole time-off thing to herself until after the festival. She wasn't sure what she would do with all that free time, maybe travel. All she knew was that she had lost her desire to plan events for other people. She had started collecting travel brochures to go over. Trish decided to talk to Jake Sullivan. He had extensive traveling experience and Trish didn't want to just see the typical tourist attractions, she wanted to understand what everyday life was like. Maybe she would write an international cook-book and collect recipes as she traveled the world. Nothing gourmet, just everyday comfort foods with easy to find ingredients. The possibilities were endless.

Chapter 18

One week before the festival Trish was in her office rushing around with Melissa and doing all the last minute planning - basically running like chickens - when Trish looked up and saw the creepy guy from the lobby staring into the window of Celebrations. He didn't even look away when Trish made eye contact with him, he just glowered at her. Hatred seemed to pour out of his pores as he stared a hole right through her. She picked-up the phone on Melissa's desk and called Davis to tell him about creepy guy. While Davis talked to security on his cell phone he briskly walked, o.k. ran, to Trish's office. By the time he got there creepy guy was on the elevator. Davis got a glimpse of him as the doors closed. He picked-up speed to try and catch the doors before they closed but just missed them. He went in Celebrations and called for Trish and Melissa.

"He's gone. I saw him but I couldn't catch him before the elevator doors closed. Are you both all right?" Davis said a little breathlessly.

"We're fine. Davis, promise me you'll never chase after him again. He was scary. He had such a look of hatred on his face today and when I looked at him he didn't even look away. He didn't start to leave until after I had hung-up the phone. Something's seriously wrong with that guy. Please let the security force or police handle him Davis." Trish was trembling as she spoke, her voice wavering as she fought to keep her jaws from chattering. Davis took her into his arms and held her, stroking her back to calm her.

"He looked like pure evil and capable of anything." she murmured as she tried to calm down. Davis' cell phone rang just as a security guard got off the elevator. He spoke a few minutes with grunts and 'uh yeah' then hung up.

"That was security. I'm going downstairs to review the security tapes from this floor to make sure these guys know who we're talking about. This guard getting off the elevator is going to plant himself in the lobby here for awhile to see if he comes back. Will you be all right, baby?" He ran his hands up and down Trish's arms and kissed her on the top of her head.

"Yeah, I'll be fine. Thank you Davis for all of this, really. I don't know what I'd do without you." Trish gently caressed Davis' cheek.

Davis fought the urge to kiss her. He wanted to take her into her office and make good use of the daybed.

"No problem. When you're ready to leave for the day, both of you, I want you to make sure someone sees you to your car. If security's busy call Larry or I and we'll do it. Got it? No negotiation on that." The security guard entered the office and Davis gave him a summary of events. He ordered him to not let Trish or Melissa out of his sight. The guard nodded and took a seat in the waiting area.

After Davis left Trish and Melissa went to talk to the security guard.

Melissa glanced at his name tag and smiled. "Duke, huh? What a great name. Is that your real name or a nickname?" Melissa asked.

"Real. My parents were big John Wayne fans."

"Cool. Duke can we get you anything to drink while you're stuck with us?" Trish asked.

"Maybe coffee if you got any."

"We do. Hot and fresh too! How do you take it?" Trish asked.

"Black."

He wasn't a real chatter box but he made them both feel safer. He was a really big guy, not fat, just big boned and very tall with a solemn, menacing look on his face. He intimidated with his size and Trish thought there was no doubt he could not only take care of himself but a small group of people single handedly.

Creepy guy didn't show up anymore that day and Duke left their office after sitting there for a couple of hours and three cups of coffee later. Trish and Melissa had been so busy they had forgotten all about the incident until Davis and Larry came into their offices at the end of the day.

Larry addressed both Trish and Davis.

"Hey, since Melissa and I were going out to dinner tonight anyway, I was wondering if you and Davis wanted to join us?"

Trish looked at Davis but couldn't read his face. She was afraid to give Davis the wrong idea, so she begged off as politely as possible.

"Oh, I don't want to intrude on your date. Melissa's probably had enough of me today. But thanks anyway for the invitation."

Trish answered nervously. The truth was Trish was afraid to go out with Davis.

She didn't trust herself around Davis. She didn't know if she could resist Davis if he were to make a move, or if she even wanted to resist. Which was exactly why she had to say no.

"Trish, come join us. You need a distraction and I don't know of a better one than Davis." Melissa asked with a pleading look on her face. "Please Trish, you look stressed and I can't help but notice you've lost more than a little weight recently. You could use a good meal and some enchanting company, but we'll go with Larry and Melissa instead. At least I'll be enchanting." T

"All right, I surrender. I know when I'm outnumbered."

Dinner turned out to be Chinese and it was delicious. Trish and Davis ate off each other's plate as if they'd been doing it all their life. Sometimes things were so easy with Davis that Trish had to remind herself that they weren't together anymore.

The one rule they all had was no shop talk. Trish started asking about travel because Larry had mentioned he had seen a number of places Trish thought she might be interested in.

"So Larry tell me all the places you've been to and which ones you liked the best and why."

"Wow. That's hard to answer. I liked a lot of countries for a lot of different reasons. Ireland is great, people are really friendly and the scenery is beautiful. The downside is the rain for us yanks as we're referred to over there. We act like we're going to melt and the natives just take it in stride and go on with their day. No big deal. Italy is another favorite, Greece I liked a lot too. I guess it depends on what you're looking for." Larry shrugged his shoulders.

"What if you don't know what you want? Just that you want to travel. What country would you recommend?" Trish questioned further.

"What's up with all the questions Trish? Are you planning on going on a trip or something?" Davis questioned.

"Well now that you ask I guess now's as good a time as any to tell you. I had planned on waiting until after the festival to say anything. I'm planning on taking an indefinite leave of absence from Celebrations. Melissa, I was planning on you running the company while I'm gone. Of course you'll get a gigantic raise

87

for it. Jake assured me he'd be available to you if you have any questions or problems." Trish tried to reassure her.

Everyone just stared at her, not saying a word. "Well now that I just broke the no work talk rule I guess I better get going. Davis, are you ready or should I call a cab? Maybe a cab would be best." Trish said as she rose from her seat and grabbed her purse.

"No, don't call a cab. I'll drive you back to your car at the office. Besides we have a rule, you leave with the person you came with, remember?"

"Some rules are made to be broken, it wouldn't be the first time one of us broke a rule." Trish said bitterly. *Man, I really do need a vacation.*

Davis ignored the insult and walked her to his car. He was willing to let it go for now but he would definitely be talking to her about it later. He was too upset to discuss it now anyway. She was planning on running away from him and he was just as determined to have her stay right where she was. If she wanted a vacation he could deal with that. After all, she worked hard and deserved a break, but he'd be dammed if this 'indefinite' bullshit wasn't going to fly. If he had to he would go to Jake and have him talk Trish out of it. *I can't lose her!*

Overall Trish had a good time. They had all been right, it felt good to go out for a change. Davis drove Trish back to her car in the parking garage of their office building. When Davis parked next to Trish's car he turned off the engine. *That's not a good sign.* She reached for the door handle.

"Trish, can we talk for a few minutes?" He looked so serious. Trish knew this couldn't be good. *Shit.* Her mind was screaming for her to get out quick but Davis didn't look like he was willing to be put off any longer.

.

"Sure, what's up?"

"I'm worried about you. You look tired, like you've pulled an all-nighter or something. You have dark circles under your eyes that make-up can't even hide anymore. You're losing weight, which tells me you're not eating regularly. You can't afford to lose any more or you'll look like a walking skeleton. And on top of all that we've got creepy guy to deal with. I'm afraid for you. I feel like you're ready to shatter into a million pieces."

"So you want to know my life plan or something? All I can tell you is that taking the time off hopefully will help get my life back on track. I really don't know what else to tell you."

"Don't leave me. Don't leave Aimee. Please, I'm begging you. I know your life hasn't been great lately but I promise you it'll get better soon. I don't want you to lose you, I just got you back." Davis had a pleading tone to his voice as he spoke.

"Davis you and Aimee lived just fine before you met me, I'm sure you'd both not only survive but thrive without me. No one's irreplaceable. I know our relationship romantically is over, but I don't think I could bear watching you be with anyone else, and yet I want nothing more than for you to be happy. For Aimee to be happy. So it's just better if I'm not around for it." Tears began to run down her cheeks.

"You're wrong about a few things. I don't want our romantic relationship to be over, that's your decision. Also, it won't be better for Aimee or I if you're not around. If you leave you'll have to deal with a stalker because I won't let you go. If you need more time to come around romantically I'll give you that but I won't let you go. Ever."

"I don't know what to say Davis. If I had been what you were looking for why did you feel the need to go out with someone else? When I ask myself that question it's the only logical conclusion I can come to."

"Look Trish I was afraid of what I was feeling for you and Aunt Sylvia pounced on that fear. She convinced me to go out, just that one time, with Sheila. She was able to convince me because I didn't trust my own judgment after my first marriage ended. That was my fault and I was afraid to make the same mistake again. I know it doesn't justify what I did, but I hope you can understand where my head was at when I agreed to go on the date. By the way, that was the date from HELL. It doesn't mean I don't care for you. It was selfish of me - stupid really. Can you please try to understand it from my point of view?"

"God Davis I can. I'm surprised it never occurred to me to look at it from any other point of view than my own. You seemed so confident.

I had no idea that you were doubting yourself or us. Why didn't you just tell me? Did you think I wouldn't understand?" Confusion consumed her and muddled her brain. She needed to think about this some more.

"I didn't understand it at the time or I certainly would have talked to you about it. Hind sight is always twenty/ twenty."

"I need to think this through all over again. But I have to tell you, right now, I feel much better. Thank you for clarifying and explaining it to me. Wow. I think I've just blown a gasket." Trish sat there, staring ahead, flabbergasted. When Trish looked at Davis she had to laugh, he looked just as stunned as Trish did.

"Well, I guess I won't be getting that sleep I need tonight either." Trish

leaned into Davis and kissed him on the lips, gently once and then more firmly the second time. Then she opened her car door and went from Davis' car to her own.

Davis waited and followed her out of the parking garage, just in case creepy guy was around. He felt like the weight of the world had been lifted from his shoulders. Trish wasn't the only one who felt better. He prayed that this was the new beginning he had hoped for with Trish.

Chapter 19

Two days before the festival and everything was ticking like a finely tuned clock. Now they were down to the physical labor of setting-up. Trish did a to scale map of all the exhibits, food booths, warming stations and she was hoping to have a dry run with the lighting people first thing tomorrow morning. So far the weather was cooperating beautifully by giving them a couple of inches of snow every day to add to the six inch base they already had.

Trish loved the way the new snow washed everything in a fresh coat of paint every day, all sparkling and new, as if fairy's had come and dusted it with pixie dust. *Stop with the fairy tales and get to work.* The only thing they were going to need the snowmaking machines for was the bunny hill for skiing. Now even Trish was excited about the festival. The chat she and Davis had in his car had changed her perspective on everything. She of all people could understand how past experiences could mold your life, for better or worse. She understood that past painful memories shaped your decisions and actions more than a person realized, similar to a knee jerk reaction to a thump on the knee cap. She had also understood that Aunt Sylvia viewed her as unsuitable for Davis and Aimee. It helped to know who your enemies were and to what lengths they would go to in getting their way. Now Davis understood his Aunt Sylvia much better and could be prepared for the next assault. Trish understood that Sylvia loved Davis and Aimee and thought she knew what was best for them. Trish just didn't have the social connections Sylvia thought were necessary for a mate or mother. Too bad. She'd have to get over that. Trish decided she wasn't giving up on Davis, so Sylvia was just going to have to deal with her.

Event day was going off without a major hitch. Trish was sure she and Melissa were going to collapse by the end of the evening. She had run across Davis, Aimee, Larry and Josie several times throughout the day. Aimee had her face painted with a picture of Romeo and had

91

gone through the mirror maze three times, probably because she liked looking at her face painting in the mirrors. Trish and Melissa shivered and cringed as they watched the men and women do the polar bear swim, some of them even stayed in the water for a whole minute before they scurried out to a waiting towel. Melissa laughed herself silly watching the little kids slipping and sliding on the ice skating rink, often watching a multi-child pile up accumulate in a matter of seconds. Some of the snow shoes were bigger than the kids wearing them as they tried to walk, let alone run, in them during the snow shoe races. Overall Trish heard a lot more laughing than crying, so that equaled success in her book. As evening fell on the festivities there was a collective sigh from the crowds as the white lights that had been strung everywhere were illuminated. The beauty of it took Trish's breath away. The crowds started to gravitate toward the pond for the grand finale fireworks when Trish heard Aimee's little voice she turned to see her and Davis standing outside the trailer that served as her temporary office. She walked toward them as she heard Aimee's desperate plea.

"But daddy I weally have to go potty." Trish, to the rescue. She took Aimee to the now empty ladies room and told Davis that 'his girls' would meet him at the pond so they could all watch the fireworks together. When they were done washing their hands and began to leave, Trish spotted creepy guy standing outside the restrooms smoking a cigarette. She froze on the spot. *Shit, now what? This guy isn't hanging around for nothing. She* tried to come up with a plan. She had to make sure Aimee was safe. They were the only ones in the bathroom. She couldn't leave a four year-old alone and knew if she tried to run with Aimee in her arms they wouldn't get very far. She pulled out her cell phone to call Davis and was surprised to see a 'no signal' message. *Great, now what?* She had to keep Aimee calm and safe. Trish knew this guy was waiting for her, not Aimee, but she wasn't sure if he knew the bathroom was empty. *Think. Think. Think.* O.k. she had a plan for Aimee's safety anyway. If this guy wanted to hurt Trish he could have done it a long time ago so there had to be another motive behind his plans. Trish showed Aimee through the open door, but at an angle so creepy couldn't see them yet they could see Davis.

"Do you see your daddy standing over there by the pond?" Trish whispered and gave Aimee the 'shhh' signal so she would whisper in response.

"Yes."

"Well, I bet I can beat you in a race to your daddy." Trish purposely
 goaded Aimee.

"No way. I'm gonna win!"

"Why don't we race and see. When you get to daddy tell him creepy guy is here by the bathroom, okay, and when I say go we'll start the race." Trish planned to place her body between the creep and Aimee. That would give Aimee a good chance of getting to Davis safely.

"Don't stop running until you get to daddy 'cause I might catch you at the last minute, I'm pretty sneaky like that." Trish was petrified as she took a deep breath and started the countdown.

 "On your mark. Get set. Go!"

They both came out of the bathroom running. Trish let go of Aimee's hand as she ran as fast as her little legs could carry her, passing Trish easily.

The next thing Trish realized was that creepy had a rag to her face. It smelled sickeningly sweet while he held her to his chest by her waist, restraining her arms at the same time. Trish sank to the ground almost instantly. She never felt creepy sweep her up into his arms, she had lost consciousness before she even hit the ground.

 Creepy picked Trish up like she didn't weigh anything, running with her to his already running car. He dumped her roughly into the backseat of the old clunker, where he bound her arms and legs then blindfolded her.

He settled himself in the driver's seat and put on his seatbelt. He knew better than to take off in a hurry, he didn't want to draw attention to himself or get stopped by the cops.

The minute Aimee reached Davis he realized Trish was nowhere to be seen Davis got a sinking feel in his stomach and the hairs on the back of his neck went up. An overwhelming feeling of doom took him over, he dialed Trish's cell phone. Listening carefully he heard her chicken dance ring coming from the direction of the bathrooms. He hastily grabbed Aimee into his arms and started to run, following the sound of Trish's phone. He found it lying on the ground under the drinking fountains

93

outside the restrooms. Trish wasn't careless about her phone, in her business it was her lifeline. He called Melissa first.

"Hey, it's Davis, do you know where Trish is?"

"No. Last time I saw her she was headed towards the bathrooms with Aimee. Is something wrong?" Melissa started getting nervous now too.

"Aimee came running to me saying she was running a race with Trish, except I can't find Trish. She would never leave Aimee. Something's wrong. I feel it. Do you know where Larry is?"

"Yeah. He's here with me. What do we do now?" Panic was setting in as Melissa grabbed Larry's hand and squeezed.

"Meet me at the bathrooms with Larry. If you'll stay here with Aimee, Larry and I will look for Trish. I found her phone on the ground outside the bathrooms."

"Shit. Shit. Shit. She would never lose her phone. Something's very wrong Davis. Do you think we should call the police?"

"Let Larry and I look for her first, we'll go from there."

When Larry and Melissa reached Davis he was holding a crying Aimee in his arms and consoling her.

"Shhhh. It's alright Aimee I'm sure Trish has a good reason for not finishing the race. Was there anyone else in the race with you two?"

"No. Twish just said that when I got to you I should tell you cweepy guy was hewe."

"Really? Did she tell you anything else sweetheart?" Davis tried to question her gently but his heart was ready to beat out of his chest now.

"No daddy. Is Twish allwight?"

"I'm sure she'll be fine honey. I want you to wait for Josie here with Melissa while Larry and I find Trish, o.k. Don't worry, everything will be

just fine." Davis gave Aimee a hug and kiss and she settled down.

"Melissa I called Josie and asked her to come and pick-up Aimee. I told her you'd be at the pond watching the fireworks and I gave her your cell phone number. Please don't let her out of your sight for a second."

"I'll keep my hands on her at all times. Try not to worry. Call me as soon as you know something."

Larry and Davis took off running in opposite directions while Melissa took Aimee's hand and walked her back to the pond.

They searched for over an hour, meeting back at the trailer. Josie had taken Aimee home and Melissa was pacing the small trailer, frantic with worry. When they walked in Melissa knew they didn't have anything good to tell her. Most everyone was gone now that the fireworks were over and the festival had ended. Melissa had gone back and checked both the men's and women's bathrooms for any sign of Trish. Nothing was there.

"Well, I'm calling the police." Davis stated.

When he talked to the police they were refusing to even take a missing persons report on her, let alone come out to the park and look for evidence. Davis knew that the longer they waited to start the investigation the colder the trail would become. Finally, frustrated beyond his limits, Davis called his Uncle Jake to see if he knew anyone who could light a fire under the police. The least they could do would be to come out and take a look around, bring some search dogs in. Davis told the police about creepy guy but they insisted they'd have to wait until Monday to talk to the security people at the office.

"That's bullshit and you know it! There's someone there twenty four seven and they have a picture of the guy - what is your fucking problem?" Davis was irate now.

"I understand your concern Mr. Sinclair but Ms. Haywood is an adult.

She could have just decided to go out of town for the weekend. People do that all the time on the spur of the moment. Does she have any family she might be visiting? Maybe you could check with them." The geek at the police department continued to give Davis a hard time.

"I'm telling you she didn't go out of town! She's the organizer of the fucking festival and she was here all day, I saw her myself. She took my four year-old daughter to the bathroom and hasn't been seen since."

"Is your daughter missing too?"

"No but Ms. Haywood gave my daughter a message telling us who took her! How many times do I have to explain this to you assholes?" Davis' face was flushed crimson red while his anger surged through him.

This was the third time he told the same cop the same story.

"Then just tell us the guy's name and we'll check it out." Idiot cop suggested.

"Let me talk to someone who understands English." Davis shouted into the phone, literally spitting with frustration. He put Davis on hold. When he came back on the lime he was much more cooperative.

"I'm going to transfer your call to Detective Kevin Chase in the missing persons division. You'll need to repeat all the information you gave me to him. He'll be in charge of the investigation from here on out. Hold on."

Davis rolled his eyes to Melissa and Larry while he told them he was being transferred to Detective Chase. He had a feeling Uncle Jake came through for him and placed the proper calls to get things moving along. When Detective Chase came on the line the only question he asked is where Davis was. He told him he was still at the trailer office in the park.

"Stay put. I'll be right there. Don't touch anything and I'll need a piece of clothing from the victim for the dogs. I'll be there in fifteen minutes."

Detective Chase hung-up quickly and was out the door, yelling over his shoulder for them to send the tracking dogs to the park.

Finally some cooperation. But it didn't make him feel any better that Trish was somewhere out there with creepy guy, alone, scared, and in danger.

Chapter 20

Trish came out of her drug induced sleep slowly, groggy and thirsty beyond anything she'd ever felt before. Her head throbbed with pain like a heartbeat. She had trouble forming a complete thought. She tried to open her eyes, only to realize she had a blindfold on. He had her

lying down on her left side with her arms tied behind her back with her ankles and knees tied together as well. She laid there trying to gather as much information as possible. Trish heard the rough running of a car engine, a really old car that also needed a muffler. She got a slight whiff of car exhaust along with the noxious stench of the car seat she was laying on. Deciding she must be in the back seat facing the trunk of the car. She tried to stay as still as possible. The longer creepy thought she was out of it the better. Trish had no idea how long she'd been unconscious but she knew her left arm and leg had fallen asleep. She used her fingers to try and figure out what materials he had used to bind her wrists. *Shit. H*e used both twine and those plastic zip type ties that the police used on criminals. He left her absolutely no wiggle room whatsoever. The plastic cut painfully into her flesh while she tested the restraints. At that moment Trish was too pissed to be scared, probably stupid of her but pissed was going to help a lot more than scared, she thought.

After what seemed like an eternity Trish heard the rhythmic clicking sound of a turn signal being used. *Great, he's a law abiding driver. No hope of being pulled over with driving like his. Where are the cops when you need 'em?* He slowed down and then turned right. When he turned Trish realized that they had been on a highway because they had been traveling at a much faster speed up until now. He wasn't accelerating very quickly. Now he drove in a stop and start pattern so Trish assumed they must be in a more populated area. She heard the thump, thump, thump of another cars bass boom while they were stopped for what Trish took for a traffic light. After multiple stops and starts, creepy began a steady increase in speed. Trish listened to the rough engine rattle and buck in protest when he pressed the accelerator harder. The loose muffler rattled under her. She felt the car vibrate and shimmy in its struggle to comply with creepy's demands. The whole time they drove creepy never touched her or said a word. Occasionally she heard him light a cigarette, smelling the smoke as it assaulted her mouth and nose. She had no idea if they were alone in the car or if someone else was in the front seat with him. One thing she was pretty sure of was that Aimee had made it to safety. She strained as she tried to remember Aimee's escape before creepy knocked her out. *God, please let her be safe.*

Trish prayed as she laid there, immobile, scared and helpless, but she was still alive and she was going to do everything in her power to stay that way. As long as creepy was still driving she felt she was safe from mortal danger. Trish kept telling herself if he wanted her dead she would already be dead, so there must be something more that he's after. But what? Money? Sex,? Torture? All those possibilities plus a few more ran through Trish's mind. Suddenly she realized whatever he was after wasn't going to be good news for her.

The situation was looking more grim as time continued to drag on. All three of them had already given their statements to Detective Chase. Davis relayed Aimee's story as well. The tracking dogs were literally running in circles. Trish had been all over that park a million times over the last week making it impossible to track her sent with any accuracy. One thing that was consistent was that they always lost the scent in the parking lot, as if she had disappeared into thin air.

Detective Chase wanted to question Aimee himself which, although Davis understood his reasoning, was hesitant to subject her to. Davis insisted that the questioning take place after Aimee woke-up in the morning with him present. Detective Chase had gotten the photo of creepy from the security office, along with copies of any video they had on him. He asked Davis and Melissa to go to the police station and look through mug shots. One thing Detective Chase knew was that creepy had done his homework very well. This guy was no idiot. All he could hope for was that he would get cocky and careless before Trish was hurt too badly. He was barking orders at some officers when his cell phone went off.

"Chase. O.k. Contact the FBI and send them over to his house, I'll be there as soon as I can." *Well at least now he knew what this was all about.*

Davis looked at Detective Chase questioningly.

"What's up?"

"The guy contacted Jake Sullivan. He didn't make any demands yet, just let him know that he had Trish and that she was still alive. Then he hung-up. We're bringing in the FBI now that it's a kidnapping. We need them to do some profiling. They're the experts on cases like this. I'm heading over to Mr. Sullivan's now. He was contacted on his personal cell, not the house phone." Detective Chase added.

"This guy must have a good understanding of technology if he got a hold of Jake's cell phone number. Jake's my uncle and only family have his private cell number. Even Trish doesn't know it. I'm going with you detective."

"No. Right now you'll do more good if you go to the station and try to identify this guy from the mug shots. I've got them at the station all ready for you. You can come over when you're done. Does Trish know Jake?" Detective Chase asked.

"Yes. Trish is the sole heir to the Haywood Lumber fortune and my uncle oversees the trust for her. He'd be the one to contact if any withdrawing from her accounts become necessary."

"Well, that explains the contact pretty well and tells me what he's after. I'll meet you at the Sullivan house when you're done at the station." Detective Chase started to walk away when Davis grabbed his arm.

"What are the chances of this having a positive outcome? Don't pull any punches."

"Historically, fifty fifty but there's always hope so don't even think about giving up. It's way too early to be thinking like that. We're just getting started, my man. I don't like to lose, so I don't." Detective Chase nodded to Davis and took off at a jog.

Davis ran his fingers through his hair in obvious frustration. Larry escorted Melissa and Davis to his car so he could take them to the police station. They drove in silence, each absorbed in their own thoughts and wracking their brains for any information that might help. Davis made a quick call to Josie and filled her in on what he knew so far. Josie agreed to stay with Aimee even though tomorrow was her day off. She reassured Davis that she would be there for Aimee for as long as it took for this to all be over. Davis asked Josie to call him when Aimee woke-up. Fear was devouring him as he sat there, helpless to do anything, waiting for any news at all. Davis' heart sank when he came to the realization that Trish had put herself in danger just to make sure Aimee was safe. That kind of sacrifice spoke volumes about how much Trish truly loved Aimee.

After hours of going through mug shots Melissa thought her eyes would cross from the strain, but she knew she had to do this for Trish. One of her best friends as well as her boss and, most importantly, a good person. Trish didn't deserve this. Melissa knew life wasn't fair but this was the first time that she understood how cruel and unfair it could be. Funny, she had always been one of those people who thought if you had money you had everything. Knowing Trish and the things she had already gone through, not to mention what she was going through right now, made her see that money could also be a curse. People with money still suffered the pain of losing a family member and still had their hearts broken. In Trish's case it was certainly working against her. She closed her eyes for a moment, trying to conjure-up the memory of creepy's face. When she opened her eyes Melissa was sure she was seeing things. She rubbed them and looked again. There he was staring back at her, creepy guy.

"Here! This Is Him! I Found Him!" Melissa screamed it at the top of her lungs.

 Davis came barreling around the desk, knocking his chair over, as he ran to her. Suddenly they were surrounded by cops as Davis looked at the picture.

"That's him!" It was all he could get out before he sat on the edge of the desk for a moment. After Davis and Melissa hugged each other Davis asked Larry to take Melissa home as he made arrangements for the police to drive him to his Uncle Jake's house.

When he entered Uncle Jake's house Davis was stunned at the number of people milling around. He asked the officer at the door where Detective Chase was and he pointed to the open library door. There he found Uncle Jake, Detective Chase and two men stringing wires around the room. Detective Chase looked up when Davis entered the room.

"Hey. I didn't expect to see you here so soon. Any news?" Chase asked.

"Yeah. Melissa spotted him in one of the books. They didn't tell you?" Davis was surprised that Detective Chase didn't know yet.

"They'll call me when they're done doing the run down on him. Might take a while if he's a known criminal. Let me show you what we're doing here. We've taken Mr. Sullivan's phone and wired it for a tap, hopefully our perpetrator will stay on long enough to track. The second wire is to catch pings off towers in case it turns out he's using a cell phone. So far we haven't heard any more from him." Detective Chase paced around the library impatiently, jiggling the change in his pocket nervously.

They all stared at the cell phone on the desk, willing it to ring. Detective Chase's phone shattered the silence when it rang. He answered and uttered a series of grunts and affirmative answer's before he hung up abruptly. Davis and Jake stared at him, clearly expecting an explanation or update of some type.

"We've got a make on the guy." He hesitated to continue until Davis spoke.

"Annnnnnd?" Davis prompted.

"Name's Sean Murdock a.k.a. Trevor McNeeley a.k.a. a half dozen other alias'. Former IRA. He's a mercenary for hire and he has quite a history, probably even worked for our government a time or two. Specializes in intelligence gathering. Proficient in electronics and explosives and an expert in survivalist situations. No known whereabouts for the last few years. Definitely operates under the radar. I wish it was better news." Detective Chase ran his hand over his face in frustration.

"So this guy's a professional then. What do you think he hopes to accomplish with all this? Trish lives very much under the radar, very modest living. She doesn't do any society type functions unless she's the event planner. Up until several weeks ago I had no idea she had money, she just doesn't give off any vibes like that. God, her idea of a wild night is a trip to the movies and a dinner out."

Davis was more worried than ever as he ran his hands through his hair for the millionth time.

"Don't think this is over-not by a long shot pal. We're contacting police departments across the entire united states to see if we can get a nibble on any information. Then, of course, the FBI is tapping their sources both nationally and internationally. We'll know something more later today. For now the balls in this assholes court."

They all sat in silence now, lost in their own thoughts.

Davis called Aimee and Josie and talked to them for a while. Josie offered to bring some clothes over for Davis which he appreciated. He hadn't had any sleep or a shower in almost forty eight hours.

Once Davis finished his conversation Jake suggested that Davis might want to look into adding more security for Aimee and Josie. Davis was ashamed that he hadn't thought to do that himself. Davis called a private security firm that Detective Chase had recommended and made immediate arrangements, then notified Josie. He made sure someone stayed at preschool with Aimee while another person stayed glued to Josie. Davis called Larry and suggested he add some private security for himself and Melissa and gave Larry an update on the situation. After a while Davis paced the room nervously, not knowing where to put himself he was so agitated and anxious. *Why hasn't the fucker called? If all he wants is money then lets just do it and get this over with, why's this guy dragging his feet?*

Chapter 21

Trish was so disoriented by now she had given up trying to figure things out. She may have even dozed off for a while, she wasn't sure of anything anymore. When she felt the car slowing down the fear leapt into her throat as she muffled her alarmed cry. Trish braced herself as she felt the car stop. When the engine was turned off she knew they had arrived, to where she had no idea. She heard a car door moan open with protest as she imagined rust falling from the hinges. The car door slammed shut with a loud groan and a thump. It sounded like a heavy door, old and creaky. She heard another door open and felt a rush of cold air coming from the direction of her feet. Still creepy said nothing. Suddenly she felt a sharp stabbing pain in her upper arm. *What the hell was that*? Trish had anticipated him touching her, but she never expected a stab with something sharp in her arm, jumping with surprise. Confusion surrounded her along with panic as she realized he had injected something into her. Terror ripped at her like sharp claws, dragging her back into unconsciousness. She tried to fight it but the drug was too strong to resist. Her last thought was of Davis and how much she loved him. Praying she would live to see him again.

When Trish woke up she was still tied as securely as she had been back in the car. Still in total darkness. Nausea overtook her and she swallowed hard trying to fight the urge to vomit. Slowly the grogginess wore off but the nausea remained. A moan escaped her when she began sweating profusely even though she was in a cold room. Underground probably, because she could smell the mustiness and feel the dampness seeping up from the floor where she lay on her back now. She smelled what she could only think of as earth. She felt the dirt floor under her hands as she dug in with her fingernails.

Cold, she was so cold her teeth began to chatter no matter how hard she tried to clinch her jaw to stop it. Trish realized she still had on her down jacket and boots but they were doing nothing to keep the cold out of her bones, her very core felt frozen solid. Something ran quickly over her body and she shuttered with revulsion. Instinct told her it had to be a mouse, it was too heavy to be a spider. *Should she risk yelling for help or even speaking at all?* Listening intently she tried her best to decipher any sound at all but all she could hear was her own heart beating wildly while her teeth continued to chatter.

If creepy guy was there with her she couldn't hear him breathing or sense any kind of motion. The air was perfectly still around her, no breezes or heat sources could be detected. Nothing but emptiness and loneliness and raw terror. Hopelessness invaded her mind as she realized she could barely roll over, let alone try to escape. For a few minutes she tried to pull her legs through her arms so they would be in front of her but she couldn't maneuver herself well enough and fell back in exhaustion from the effort. Either she was really out of shape, or still under the effects of whatever drugs he had pumped into her, because every effort seemed monumental to her. Her efforts did pay off in one way, she was now sure she was alone because no one had tried to stop her lame escape attempt. At once she was both comforted and scared at the thought that she was alone and underground. There was nothing to do now but wait and shiver off the cold. Although her nausea was beginning to subside she was now so thirsty she couldn't conjure enough saliva to even wet her lips.

What seemed like hours later Trish heard someone open a creaky door and come down a set of wooden steps with heavy thumping shoes. Once they reached the bottom of the steps the footfalls were much softer and harder for her to hear, terrified now because she didn't know where he was or what would be coming at her. She steeled her spine, anticipating some sort of pain or another needle being stuck into her. Someone grabbed her by the back of her coat collar, without a word, and pulled her into a sitting position, propping her against what her fingers told her was a dirt wall. Of all the things Trish could have expected, it certainly wasn't the sound of Darth Vader telling her to take a drink of water. When she felt the plastic touch her lips she obeyed immediately. Trish gulped greedily at the water for as long as she could before he took the bottle from her lips.

"What do you want from me?"

He answered her with a hard punch to her jaw, sending her back down to the ground as she hit her head on the hard dirt floor.

Creepy responded in his Darth Vader voice.

"You will speak only when asked to, or I will gag you." Then Trish felt the now familiar stab of a needle in her thigh. Her ears were still ringing from the blow to her head when she heard his heavy footsteps going back up the stairs, pausing after only a few steps for a moment before pushing what sounded like a heavy door open. The thump of the door closing made her heart sink. Then silence once again, as sleep overcame her.

By the time Jake's cell phone rang Davis had been dozing in the chair of the library. He jumped, suddenly wide awake. He looked around the room as Detective Chase and some FBI guy motioned for Jake to answer it. Jake knew to keep him on the phone as long as possible. They were sure creepy knew all the tricks of the trade but they still had to try.

"Hello."

"I want five million dollars transferred to an account of my choosing. Get the funds ready and I'll call back with the details. She is alive and unhurt, lets keep it that way."

Then they heard a loud click as he hung up the phone. A voice changer had been used just like the police had told him it would be. He had used it on his previous call, Darth Vader. *How appropriate.*

The call had been way too short to do a land line trace so they had to rely on ping's off cell phone towers to try and track the call. The police knew within a few minutes that the asshole had used a non-traceable cell phone or a signal scrambler because they only had a couple pings before they lost the call.

Jake knew he was supposed to demand to talk to Trish but the guy never gave him a chance. So now they were back to waiting again. Davis asked Detective Chase if there was any news about creepy's location but he already knew the answer as Chase just shook his head. About an hour later Detective Chase and the FBI agent were called out of the room. Davis looked hopefully at Jake and Jake just shrugged his shoulders.

When Davis stood and looked out the library doors he was surprised to see Aunt Sylvia with a tray of sandwiches she was passing around to everyone. He also noticed there was a bar full of refreshments for everyone to help themselves to as well. Now wasn't she being the sweet little hostess. Davis knew it wouldn't look good if Sylvia didn't do something to help. *After all she had a reputation to uphold.* He tried to rein in his anger at Sylvia for having robbed him of so much time with Trish. Sylvia was aware that Davis had be angry with her for all her interference and manipulation. She was sure Trish must hate her and had made a point of avoiding her whenever she visited Jake's office. A simple apology could never repair the damage that she had done but she knew she should have at least tried. An error that she was determined to correct once Trish was back safe and sound. Sylvia noticed Davis and approached with the tray in hand. As he took a sandwich he murmured his thank you.

"Davis I'm so sorry this is happening. You know I've always liked Trish and I hope everything works out for the best. Can I get you anything else dear?"

"No. Thank you Aunt Sylvia." Davis turned back into the library to eat his sandwich. He had no idea what kind of sandwich it was, just that it filled his stomach, and he wondered if Trish was hungry right now. She had already lost too much weight as it was. She couldn't stand to lose much more. Davis visibly shook himself as he tried to keep a positive attitude, which was becoming harder and with each passing moment. Detective Chase walked briskly back into the room.

"Okay here's the latest update. The FBI has a lead from an informant about where he may be holding Trish and they're following-up on that. It corresponds with the pings we got off some cell towers before the guy scrambled his signal. The phone was a throw away so we can't completely trace it. We're starting to close the net a little." He said excitedly.

"Oh, one more thing. They finished analyzing the tape of the last call and didn't find any background noises."

"Where do they think he's holding her?" Davis asked.

"Somewhere outside of Boston. We know this for a few reasons. One is the informant, two is the fact that there are no background noises, telling us he's not in the city, and finally based on the hours elapsed since the abduction he couldn't have gotten too far outside of Boston by then. We're guessing that he followed the traffic laws to a tee because we have no record of any stops or speeding tickets being issued during the travel timeframe that match his description."

"I want to be there when they find her. She's going to be scared and I want to be there. I'll charter a plane myself. Do you want to come with me Detective?" Davis felt hope for the first time since this whole thing started.

"Hold on a minute Davis, I know you want to help but let's just wait a little to see what the agents in Boston have to say. This could be a wild goose chase."

Detective Chase tried to settle Davis down a bit but Davis wasn't having any of it.

"I don't care if I have to spend the next three days on a fucking plane traveling around the country, I need to be there when they find her. You need to understand that I'm not asking your permission, I'm telling you I'm going. Now, do you want a ride or not? Uncle Jake, do you know anybody at the Boston FBI headquarters that we can talk to?" Finally Davis felt like he could do something other than wait and twiddle his thumbs. They were going to find her, his gut told him they were on the right trail.

"Yes. I know the director. I'll make sure someone meets your plane when you land at the airport."

Maybe Aunt Sylvia had a point about those social contacts she was always harping about.

"Great. Thanks. Detective are you coming?" Davis asked as he grabbed his coat and pulled out his phone to make the flight arrangements.

"Um, yeah. I'd like to be in on this to the end. Thanks"

"Let's go." Davis sped out the door as Detective Chase motioned Davis toward his car. They drove with the sirens on and at full speed, Detective Chase on the phone the whole time and gathering more details.

Chapter 22

When the plane landed in Boston there was an FBI agent waiting for them just as Jake had promised. Davis and Detective Chase raced out of the plane to the waiting agent, making their introductions on the run towards the car. "I'm Detective Kevin Chase and this is Davis Sinclair, he's the victim's fiancee."

"I'm Agent Weiss, nice to meet you. We've had some activity since I last spoke to you. We have surveillance in position at the location our informant indicated and there is a car parked there. According to our informant this farm hasn't had any occupants in the last year, so hopefully we're onto something. One of the agents was able to get close enough to the vehicle and felt the hood, it was still a little warm. That can be a good sign. I've been told to take you both to the location and see if Mr. Sinclair can make a positive I.D. on the guy."

"Has there been any activity since the agents took their positions?" Detective Chase asked.

"Not that I'm aware of."

"How far is this place and what kind of place is it?" Davis asked.

"It's about another fifteen minutes outside of town and it's an abandon horse farm, apparently the owner died last year and had no heir, so it's sat vacant until the rest of the family gets done fighting over it."

Agent Weiss stomped on the gas pedal as they raced toward the farm. When they reached the farm it was pitch black outside, not even a sliver of the moon shone through the clouds. Agent Weiss handed Davis and Detective Chase each a flashlight and asked them to keep them off until further notice. Davis moved into the hedgerow the other agents were using for cover and crouched down, waiting for the agents to make their move. A scout sent out to look around reported at least one male inside the residence sleeping on the couch in the living room with a rifle by his side. No one was seen inside the barn or shed. No sightings of Trish. She was here somewhere, Davis felt it in his bones.

After some discussion the agents decided to storm the house and barn simultaneously and, when the all clear was given, Davis and Detective Chase were going into the barn to search for Trish while another group of agents would search the house.

The agents approached the buildings in complete silence and stealth. On agent Weiss' signal they knocked in the door while yelling FBI freeze! In short order Davis and Detective Chase were given the all clear sign and they ran into the barn with their flashlights blazing.

The barn was rather bare, with each horse stall empty except for one which held some bails of hay or straw or whatever the hell it was. There was no sign of Trish anywhere. In an effort to settle down Davis sat on the hay bail, disappointed and exhausted. He couldn't believe his gut had been wrong. They had to be missing something. Davis went into the house and verified creepy's identity. Apparently he was refusing to talk. All Davis could think of was killing the bastard. Davis started to dive for him but Detective Chase grabbed him in a bear hug to restrain him. The suspect just turned to Davis and gave him a big shit eating grin while the agent's led him out of the house to their waiting car. Davis went back to the barn to try and get himself under control when he heard a commotion and a gunshot out by the cars. Davis hesitated a moment before he stooped down and looked out the open barn doors. He saw creepy lying on the ground in a pool of blood, eyes wide open in a fixed stare, the stare of death. Davis staggered back into the barn and sat on one of the bales of hay. Dejected, he tried to gather his thoughts as he let his flashlight fall to the ground. He held his head in his hands. When he followed the beam of the flashlight he saw an old metal hinge on the barn floor attached to a piece of wood. On a hunch, he moved the bale of hay that lay on top the wood, stunned to see a trap door with a deadbolt. *Could this be real or was he dreaming?* He slid the bolt and opened the creaky door. Shining his flashlight through the opening he saw some stairs which he ran down as fast as possible, almost falling face first onto the dirt floor. He shined his flashlight around the room and finally spotted a booted foot. His heart soared as he raced to Trish's shivering body. He grabbed her into his arms and removed her blindfold as he checked her vital signs.

"Trish oh baby, it's me Davis. Honey open your eyes for me. Please baby try to wake-up." Trish just moaned and shivered as Davis yelled for someone, anyone, to come help.

"Hey! I've Got Her! Down Here In The Barn! Hurry! We Need An Ambulance Right Away! Davis frantically started rubbing Trish's arms and legs as Detective Chase came running to Davis. Immediately he started to cut through Trish's bindings. As soon as she was free Davis scooped her up into his arms and ran up the steps with her. He saw agent Weiss and ran full speed to him.

"Come on Weiss we don't have time to wait for an ambulance, we need to take her now!" Detective Chase followed Davis at a run and opened the passenger side door for Davis. Weiss slid behind the wheel and put his siren on, driving as fast as humanly possible to the nearest hospital.

Davis never stopped talking to Trish the entire ride. He stroked her face and body and kissed her in between sentences.

"Come on Trish I need you to stay with me. Don't you dare leave me now, do you hear me? I'm not letting you go so you're just going to have to deal with it." Davis repeated over and over. Trish finally murmured in a barely audible tone.

"Davis? Where's Aimee? Is she alright? Am I dreaming?"

Excited, Davis hugged her hard against his chest.

"No baby you're not dreaming, I'm here. Aimee's fine thanks to you, baby."

Davis wasn't sure how much Trish understood, she had lapsed back into her sleepy state, but she was o.k. and that was all that mattered.

When Weiss had barley come to a stop in front of the Emergency Room doors Davis bolted out of the car and into the reception area. A waiting gurney was pushed over to him as he gently placed her onto it. When Davis followed the staff into the treatment room he was asked to wait in the waiting room.

"No disrespect intended, but no fuckin' way. I stay. Period." Davis moved to the head of the gurney.

"Are you a family member?" A nurse asked.

"Yes. I'm her fiancee. I don't know if you're aware but she's been the victim of a kidnapping, so lets stop wasting time and you go get the fucking doctor."

Davis was getting pissed, ready to go hunt the doctor down himself if necessary. The nursing staff cut-off all of Trish's clothes as Davis pulled off her boots. The doctor came rushing into the room and seeing Trish shivering uncontrollably he barked an order for some heated blankets to be put on her immediately. Davis had a feeling he was going to like this guy.

Dr. Eric Samuels, according to the name on his lab coat, didn't say anything as he examined Trish. A grunt here and a 'humph' there was all he committed to while the nurse relayed all the information she knew about Trish's situation.

"And this is her fiancee. He has refused to leave the room." Disapproval was dripping from her statement as she looked Davis in the eyes.

Tough shit lady.

When Dr. Samuels finished his exam he ordered some blood drawn and some x-rays before he turned his attention to Davis.

"Hi I'm Dr. Samuels and you are?"

"Davis Sinclair. Nice to meet you. How is she?"

"Well, what I can tell you so far is she seems a little hypothermic right now and, as you can see, she's shivering. She has some bumps and bruises on her face and head and we'll x-ray those to make sure there's no fracture. It's going to take a while to warm her back to the correct body temp. But I don't see any signs of frostbite so that's a positive. Her pupils tell me she's been drugged within the last forty eight hours. If you combine all of that with what she's been through I'm sure shock is probable as well. As you heard, I ordered additional tests, just as a precaution, make sure she doesn't have any fractures and to identify the drugs she was given. Overall her prognosis is excellent and I would expect a full recovery unless something else turns up in the tests. I thought I detected a little fluid in her lungs so I'm putting her on a antibiotic as a precaution against pneumonia. All her vital signs are good considering her condition. She seems a little dehydrated so we started an I.V. and she's more than a little malnourished. That didn't just happen in the last two days, she needs to eat more and regularly. We'll be admitting her as soon as her tests are completed. Do you have any questions?"

"How long do you think it will be until I can take her home?" Davis wanted to go, Now!

"I don't want to rush things here. I know you're anxious to get her home but I would say probably in a couple days, as long as her tests come back alright. I'll have a better idea after the blood tests. We'll talk about discharge then."

111

"Thank you Dr. Samuels. I appreciate everything you've done for her." Relief poured out of Davis' body as he absorbed all the information the doctor had given him. *She was going to be alright!* Davis sent up a little prayer of thank you.

"Now here's a little bit of free medical advice from me to you. You look like shit man. You need to eat and sleep so you're well enough to take care of her. It won't be just the physical that will need tending, mentally she'll end up needing even more support than physically."

"That's very sound advice and I appreciate it, but I'm not leaving her side. Do you have a room for two? I promise no hanky panky." Davis smiled but made it clear he meant every word as he held her hand and stroked her arm.

"I'll make some arrangements for it." Dr. Samuels made a face at the nurses disapproving glare as he left the room.

While Trish was in x-ray Davis talked with Detective Chase and made arrangements for his private plane to take him back to Harbor Springs. Davis had just one other question for him.

"What about Sean Murdock? What happens now?"

"Apparently Mr. Murdock tried to run from custody and attempted to get one of the officers guns. In the struggle Mr. Murdock was shot and subsequently died en route to the hospital. It appears money was his sole motivation and that he acted alone."

"Yeah. That's the same thing they said about the Kennedy assassination. I think I'll keep our security in place now that I know there are nuts like him running around. Can you tell me if everyone back home knows that Trish has been found and everything is fine?" Davis felt the need to call everyone but didn't want to leave Trish long enough to make the calls. Hospitals didn't like cell phones very much.

"They've all been informed, except possibly your nanny and daughter. Maybe you'd like to handle that yourself." Detective Chase smiled.

"I'll stay here with Ms. Haywood while you call from the lobby."

Davis dashed into the lobby and made the world's fastest phone call to Josie. Aimee was so upset about Trish that Josie let her fall asleep in front of the television while her favorite Disney video played. He promised to call back first thing in the morning and gave Josie permission to let her stay on the couch as long as she wanted. Trish was just being wheeled out of x-ray when Davis got back. As Detective Chase headed out the door he turned and asked Davis one last question

."Are you really her fiancee?"

"I will be as soon as she's awake." Davis took Trish's hand and kissed it gently.

Chapter 23

Trish came awake slowly. It felt wonderful to finally be warm again. She was afraid to open her eyes, thinking she was dreaming. If her eyes opened the dream would be over and she'd be cold again. She tested her theory by moving her legs slightly. When they weren't bound any longer she slowly opened her eyes. The first thing she saw was Davis sleeping peacefully next to her in her bed. Her heart leapt with happiness to realize he was here with her. He looked exhausted. His beautiful hair was tousled and his handsome face had a few days worth of beard stubble. He looked so peaceful sleeping next to her, hugging the side of the bed to give her as much room as possible. Thank God for the railing or he'd be on the floor. He was fully dressed and on top the covers, although someone had thrown a blanket over his legs in an attempt to keep him warm.

Trish gently took his hand to her mouth and kissed it, trying not to wake him. Her heart was full of love, pure, unequivocal, straight forward love. Never had she felt so at peace as she did at this moment, or so safe. She tried to remember how she had gotten here, wherever here was. Obviously a hospital but she had no idea which hospital. The last thing she remembered was being stabbed with a needle.

Trish felt an overwhelming need to tell Davis, finally, that she loved him. It didn't matter if he loved her or not. Life was too short to waste time with useless emotions of pride or hurt. Fear, true, life altering, fear was no excuse for holding back her feelings. She rubbed her fingers lightly over his hand, caressing it lovingly until he slowly came awake.

The minute his eyes opened he saw his beautiful Trish. He smiled as he raised his hand to caress her bruised cheek.

"Hey, beautiful. Welcome back. I missed you. Hope you don't mind the company in your bed, I just had to hold you, to be with you."

"Davis, I love you. I had to say that because through this whole thing all I could think about was that I had never told you that I loved you. I don't want you to feel uncomfortable and I don't expect you to say it back, I just needed to tell you." She rushed through her statement, mostly from nerves.

"Oh, baby you don't know how much I've wanted to tell you how much I love you. I was afraid if I did I'd scare you off. Trish, I love you. I realized another thing too through all this. I want to spend the rest of my life with you, will you please do me the honor of marring me?"

"Davis are you sure you're not just upset? Maybe we should wait on that answer until you're sure, you know, not still in this situation. Until you've had time to think this through."

"What do you think I've been doing this whole time? All I could think of was how much I loved you. I can't imagine life without you. I loved you before all this happened and now I simply refuse to live without you. I'm ready for our happily ever after. We both deserve to be happy but that won't happen until we're married. Please, marry me."

"Absolutely, positively, yes, yes, yes, YES!" Trish yelled happily in between kisses, long luxurious kisses.

When the nurse came into the room she quickly put a stop to their kisses and kicked Davis no only out of the bed, but out of the room. Davis paced nervously in front of the closed door, anxious to get back to Trish. He made a quick call to Melissa, letting her know that Trish was awake and doing well. He also laid the marriage news on her and set the wheels in motion for the wedding. He trusted Melissa to take care of the rest.

When the nurse finally let Davis back into Trish's room she had been showered, poked, prodded and monitored into exhaustion. She tried to fight off the sleep but Davis insisted she close her eyes and sleep. They had the rest of their lives ahead of them but only if she got well enough to leave the hospital. He assured her he wasn't going anywhere.

"Good luck trying to get rid of me now, future Mrs. Sinclair, you'd have to blast me out of here. Sleep my love, I promise I'll be here when you wake up." Davis stroked Trish's hair until she fell asleep. When the nurse came in Davis asked for a pair of scrubs so he could shower and change. After his shower, he laid on the bed next to Trish and drifted off to sleep himself, completely content, as he held Trish in his arms. Joy consumed him as his last thought was that this was the way he and Trish would fall asleep every night from now on, together.

When Trish woke from her nap she found Davis once again by her side, asleep, with his arms around her and his face buried in her neck. The nurse entered the room and to Trish's surprise she gently shook Davis awake.

"Mr. Sinclair you have some visitors." She patted his shoulder as he startled awake.

"Did you hear me Mr. Sinclair, you have some visitors."

"Oh, right. I'll be right there." He mumbled as he gave Trish's forehead a quick kiss and got off the bed.

"Davis, who would be visiting you here?"

"Umm, I'm not sure, let me go see. I'll be right back. Don't go anywhere."

Davis returned about ten minutes later. When he walked in she heard a little giggle. When Davis reached the bed Aimee jumped out from behind him, giggling wildly .

"SUPWISE!"

"Oh my God Aimee I'm so happy to see you. How'd you get here? Where's Josie? You really, really surprised me!" Trish was so relieved to see her, happy and healthy. She didn't seem traumatized at all. Davis had told her she was fine but Trish was glad to see it for herself.

"Come right over here and give me a big hug and kiss. I've missed you so much. I love you my little Aimee."

Aimee did as Trish asked leading off with the traditional raspberries followed by the kiss. She wrapped her arms around Trish's neck, hugging her tightly.

"Daddy had his aiwplane come and get me and Josie to visit you!"

"I'm so glad. Did you have fun on the airplane?"

"Uh huh. We wewe way up in the sky with the clouds." Aimee stretched her arms above her head as she spoke.

Trish took Davis' hand and squeezed it as he sat on the bed with them.

"Thank you so much for getting her here Davis. It makes me feel a lot better to see for my own eyes that she's just as beautiful as I remembered."

Davis took Trish's hand as he kissed her lips, lingering a little too long according to Aimee.

"Daddy, that's too long. Twish needs to bweathe."

Both of them burst out laughing as a nurse came into Trish's room pushing a wheelchair.

"Time to take a little trip, Ms. Haywood. Hop on board while I grab your I.V. and hook it up on the pole for you."

"Where are we going?"

"Oh, you'll see." The nurse smiled for the first time Trish could remember.

The nurse pushed the wheelchair as Aimee and Davis followed down the hospital hall way. When they reached the door labeled Lounge Trish turned and looked at Davis. She could see by the look on his face that he was up to something.

"Davis, what are you up to?"

"Me? What could I possibly be up to?" He pretended to be innocent but Trish knew better. She quickly changed tactics.

"Aimee, did daddy tell you what he's up to?"

"I'm not allowed to tell." She said somberly. Wild horses couldn't drag the information from her as she pinched her lips shut to prove her point. Aimee looked at Davis and he winked at her in approval. When the doors opened Trish couldn't believe her eyes.

The room was set up like a wedding chapel. Flowers sat on either side of an arbor where a man Trish didn't know stood with a bible in his hands. Now Trish realized he wore the collar of a clergy member. Standing around the arbor were Melissa, Larry, Jake Sullivan, Sylvia Sullivan, Josie, and Duke the security guard. They were all smiling broadly and watching Trish's reaction. Slowly it dawned on Trish what was going on and she looked lovingly at Davis. Tears moistened her eyes as she was overcome with happiness.

"Well you said you'd marry me and I decided we'd wasted enough time already. I won't take the chance that you'll change your mind."

"Never. Davis, I love you and it's perfect. Everyone we care about is here and that's what's important. I'm not understanding the Duke thing, but we'll save that for another time. He's a nice guy and welcome to share our day with us."

"Duke is now your personal bodyguard. I hired him yesterday away from the security company at the office building. Melissa said he worked out good for you two so I figured it would be alright. All of us now have twenty four seven security. This is Never happening again."

117

"Welcome to the family Duke. Thank you for coming to our wedding." Trish smiled broadly but jumped at the pain in her jaw, reminding her that she still had some recovering to do. Trish began to stand but Davis put his hand on her shoulder.

"Nope, you stay there." He kneeled next to Trish and nodded to the pastor.

"We're ready pastor. Let's do this."

The ceremony took only a few minutes but would last a lifetime. She stayed and mingled with her guests. This was the best wedding she'd ever been to, and she had been to more than her fair share.

At this wedding she actually got to sit and visit with everyone, no photographer was constantly poking and posing her and Davis. Okay, the food could have been better, hospital food being what it was. Aimee sat on Trish's lap as they wheeled around the room with Davis doing the steering. There were times they felt like they were on a ride in an amusement park the way Davis twirled them. All too soon it was came to a close.

"Well, I can't thank everyone enough for coming, all of you are here because Trish and I love you and are grateful to all of you. But as you can see, I need to get my bride back to bed." He wiggled his eyebrows wildly as everyone laughed.

"Melissa this would never have happened without you. Thank you for putting all of this together for us. Trish will do the same for you someday." He directed his gaze straight at Larry as he paused.

"Aimee, daddy and your new mommy will be home in a couple of days so you be a good girl for Josie, okay? We love you baby." Davis leaned down and raspberried and kissed her and then Trish followed up with the same routine.

Davis whirled Trish around and back to her room. The nurse helped get her settled back into her bed and ran a routine check of her vital signs. When she left Davis crawled into her bed and laid next to her, taking her into his arms and kissing her lovingly, over and over again. He couldn't get enough of her and he thought he never would. Trish wrapped her arms around his neck and pressed the length of her body against his kissing him back eagerly. Davis backed off when his arousal became almost too much for him to control.

"Don't you want to consummate our marriage?" Trish asked with a husky voice.

"I would but you're such a screamer during sex. I don't want everyone running in here when you orgasm. It could be embarrassing."

"What if I promise to stick a washcloth in my mouth to muffle the scream, would that work for you?"

The whole time Trish spoke she was removing Davis' clothing. Slowly tickling his skin with the light strokes of her fingers. When she untied his scrub bottoms she slipped her hand inside the waistband and cupped his arousal, fondling him lovingly, wanting to put him in her mouth as she licked her lips. That threw Davis into frantic action as he ravaged Trish, hoping the wheels on the bed were locked so they wouldn't go cruising all over the room. Trish buried her face into Davis' neck as she came over and over again, trying to muffle her cries of pleasure. Davis entered her with one hard thrust, fighting to stay quiet as his thrusts quickened until he exploded with pleasure.

Chapter 24

Two Months Later

After two months of marriage life began to settle down for the Sinclair family. Trish had cut down quite a bit on her hours at the office, sharing some of the responsibilities with Melissa. Now that Melissa was so much busier Duke had even started pitching in. He didn't have to, but there were days he was bored he had learned more than he ever wanted to admit about planning a wedding. Boy, some women were freaking crazy lunatics when it came to their weddings. He didn't know how Trish and Melissa managed to keep their cool sometimes.

Three days per week Trish worked only until two in the afternoon so she could spend time with Aimee. Trish loved her time with Aimee as she got to know all her little habits and quirks. Her bedtime routine was an exact process every night, no exceptions, no substitutions. First dinner, then she had her bath with a different toy in the bath each day to prevent boredom. Once the bath was over it was brush her hair and teeth and then select a sleeping buddy to take to bed. Once she was tucked in by Davis and Trish, a story was read with both Davis and Trish taking turns reading. Raspberries then the kiss and it was nightie night. Quiet, alone time for Trish and Davis. Her favorite time of the day.

Sometimes they would lay on the couch in each other's arms and read and listen to music. Other times they would pop in a dvd and cuddle on the couch, but most nights they just went straight to bed themselves talking and making love throughout the night, safe in each other's arms. Marriage agreed with both of them just fine. Davis appreciated the way Trish had made room in her life for both him and Aimee. They were clearly her priority and she made sure they felt loved above all else. Her career was important to her but would never take the place of her family. To Trish it wasn't a sacrifice at all, but pure pleasure. Davis and Aimee had made her feel loved and welcome from the minute she entered their home.

It started out as a normal day, breakfast with Aimee, Trish and Davis driving to work together then going their separate ways with a kiss in the hallway. Duke and Melissa having their first cup of coffee together, staring at the walls and not saying a word to each other until the caffeine kicked in. Trish knew better than to say anything to either of them until the coffee did its magic. Trish was a morning person, even more so now that she had Aimee in her camp, but she knew morning people pissed-off night people so she tried to keep a low profile until Melissa spoke in a complete sentences.

Sylvia was coming into the office to plan Davis and Trish's wedding reception with all her society friends, trying to deflect rumors of a forced wedding because of an unplanned pregnancy. Normally Trish could care less what people thought, but after her kidnapping Davis convinced her that without those social contacts of Jake and Sylvia's they wouldn't even take a missing persons report, let alone have found her. So today she would paint on a smile and let Sylvia go at it, anything she wanted she would get, it was the least she could do for all their help and to keep Sylvia off Davis' back.

Sylvia breezed into Celebrations promptly at ten o'clock looking like spring itself in her light blue suit with pastel scarf. Melissa snapped to attention and Duke straightened himself in his chair in reaction to Sylvia, most people did that around Sylvia, she had that kind of presence.

"Trish, Melissa, Duke how are you today? Have you looked outside? It looks like a beautiful spring day, I even saw a robin this morning."

"Yes, I can't wait for spring-it's been a long winter this year." Trish said pleasantly. "Can I get you a refreshment before we begin, Sylvia. I thought it might be best if we worked in the conference room today, will that be alright with you?"

"No nothing for me darling, thank you. The conference room will be just fine with me." Sylvia had decided to be as agreeable as possible today, no matter what ideas were presented to her. Sylvia turned and headed toward the conference room as Trish followed, looking like she was going to her own execution. Trish counted the hours until she and Sylvia were scheduled to meet with Davis and Jake for lunch.

"Before we begin Trish I just want to say how sorry I am to have interfered in your and Davis' relationship by setting-up that date with Sheila. Davis didn't want to but I pushed it on him without any thought to how it would affect anyone." Sylvia said as she laid her hand softly on Trish's arm, then gave a little squeeze.

"Sylvia the way I see it we both love Davis and Aimee and we both want to see them happy. With a team like us, how can we go wrong? Do you think we could start over now that we have a goal of making Davis and Aimee happy?"

"Absolutely! Oh, thank God. I feel so much better now. Believe it or not I was so nervous coming here today."

"I feel better too. So tell me what did you have in mind for the reception?"

Once Sylvia and Trish got their groove on there was no stopping them, and Trish was surprised that she was actually enjoying herself. Before lunch they had decided on the venue, color scheme, menu. The guest list Trish was leaving up to Sylvia. Both Trish and Sylvia felt a sense of accomplishment when they left to meet Davis and Jake for lunch.

The minute Trish saw Davis' face she knew something was terribly wrong. His brow was furrowed in an angry scowl and Jake didn't look pleased either. Trish leaned into Davis' ear and whispered.

"Is everything o.k.? You don't look too happy. What's wrong?"

Davis just looked at her and whispered back

"I'm fine. Everything's fine." Trish didn't buy it for a minute.

Sylvia ignored their expressions and started babbling on and on about the plans they had already completed. Trish grabbed Davis' hand underneath the table and squeezed lightly while Sylvia chattered away. He barely glanced at her, preoccupied with his own thoughts. Trish had never seen Davis like this before. She desperately wanted to talk to him but couldn't think of a way to get him alone. She'd have to wait until their drive home to find out what the problem was.

When lunch was over Trish and Sylvia headed back to her office to finish-up their plans. Invitations still had to be selected along with centerpieces, entertainment and table linens. Sylvia hesitated as if she was afraid to bring up what was on her mind and Trish caught the hesitation.

"There's something you're not telling me Sylvia. What is it that we've forgotten?"

"Well it's not that we've forgotten but rather something I was hoping you'd consider doing."

"Shoot. I'm open to almost anything." Trish answered, her body language echoed her thoughts with her palms facing up and hands fully open.

Sylvia decided to dive in head first.

"I was hoping you and Davis would consider repeating your vows at the hall in front of everyone."

"I think that's an absolutely lovely idea. I never pictured myself getting married in a hospital, let alone in a hospital gown. Of course if we're going to do that I would have to insist that Aimee attend and be included in the ceremony. I couldn't get married without her being there, especially if this is going to be more like a fairy tale. Do you have a problem with that?"

The look of shock on Sylvia's face made Trish laugh.

"Oh my, I never thought you would go along with it. I'm so happy. Thank you for giving me this and of course Aimee would have to be included."

"With these new developments I'll need a more formal dress than I had originally planned, would you mind helping me pick one out? I'd like Melissa to stand as my maid of honor and Aimee as my flower girl so we'll need dresses for them too."

Sylvia burst into tears and Trish ran around the table to hug her.

"What's wrong? Did I do something to offend you? If I did I'm so sorry." Trish was panicked now.

"No, no. Not at all, in fact, just the opposite. I was so wrong about you not being suitable for Davis and I'll spend the rest of my life regretting that. I would be honored to help you with the dresses."

"Great! I'll find a good time for Melissa and give you a call, we'll make a day of it."

By the time Sylvia left Trish was exhausted both physically and mentally and decided to take five minutes on the daybed in her office before she got back to work. The next thing she knew Davis was gently shaking her shoulder and calling her name.

"Davis! What time is it? Is everything alright?" She had popped-up like a jack-in-the-box, startled.

"Shhhh. It's okay, you fell asleep and it's time to go home. Do you feel alright?" Davis checked Trish's head for a temperature.

"Yeah, I'm fine. I was tired after spending the day with Sylvia so I laid down for what was supposed to be five minutes and I must have fallen asleep. I'm losing it Davis. I've never done this before in my life, but I feel fine. Let's go home." Trish sat up and put her shoes back on. They walked out with Melissa and Duke in tow.

Trish noticed Davis still had an angry look on his face as he maneuvered through traffic.

"Davis you look worried, or angry or something, is everything o.k.?"

"I'm fine. Everything's fine."

"Are you sure, because I noticed it at lunch today too. It's like you're in your own little world, you know, distracted." Trish wasn't letting this go.   Something was big time wrong but he didn't want to talk about it, not now and not with Trish.

 "Davis I hope it's alright with you but after lunch your Aunt Sylvia asked if we would renew our wedding vows at the hall during our reception. I told her we would. Are you o.k. with that?"

"Really? You'd do that for her?"

"Yeah. I'd do it everyday for the rest of my life if you wanted me to. I love you and I'm proud to let everyone know how much I love you. Some people need to see the vows to believe it's real."

"I love you and I love the idea."

"Great! I've already talked to Melissa about being my maid of honor and Aimee will be our flower girl. It should be fun and I think Aimee will love the whole fairy tale aspect of it. Sylvia agreed to help me pick out my dress and Melissa's, we're making a day of it."

"Sounds like things went well between you and Sylvia today."

"Oh Davis it went so much better than I expected. We apologized to each other about past hurt feelings and decided to start fresh and I feel like we really did. I don't see the point in denying her anything about the reception because we're doing it mainly for her, so why shouldn't she get her way? So far she's been very reasonable, in my opinion."

"Have I told you how much I love you today?"

"About three minutes ago."

"That long ago? Really? Let me say it again then, I love you."

Chapter 25

As the wedding and reception moved closer and closer Trish had a sinking feeling as Davis became more upset and secretive. He was worried about something that he refused to discuss with Trish and that made her worry even more. She asked on many occasions if it was something she had done but he always denied it had anything to do with his home life. On top of that Trish had not been feeling herself lately, attributing it to stress so she kept it to herself. She made a note to herself to ask Melissa for a referral to a doctor, she was probably low in iron or something. Finally a few days later, after having a very bad day at the office, Trish snapped.

"Davis you need to tell me what's wrong right now. I can't take this silence anymore. You've shut me out, which makes me believe it has something to do with me. Spill it." She crossed her arms over her chest.

"Really, it's nothing."

"Well Davis I have a news flash for you, I'm not stupid and I know something's wrong. It hurts me to think you don't trust me enough to tell me. The only conclusion I can come to is that it concerns me, otherwise you'd tell me."

Trish got up and went into the spare bedroom to be alone as she burst into tears. The more upset she got the more nauseous she got until she was running for the bathroom and vomiting. Davis heard the commotion and came running into the bathroom to see what was wrong.

"Oh baby, are you sick? I'm sorry I didn't know you weren't feeling good. What can I do to help?"

"Go away! I'm fine. There's nothing wrong with me."

"What are you talking about, you're throwing up in the goddamn toilet!"

"Now you know how I feel when you shut me out and deny that anything's wrong. Just forget it Davis, you apparently don't want to share your life with me. Go away and let me puke in peace." She was crying now and as white as a sheet. When she was done she went back to the guest bedroom and fell asleep.

125

She slept through dinner and through the night. When she woke Davis was sleeping beside her. When she turned to face him his eyes open.

"I'm sorry, you're right there is something wrong and I didn't want you to worry so I kept it to myself. My ex-wife showed up at the law office on the day you and Sylvia met Jake and I for lunch. She told me that she wants another payment for staying away from Aimee and if she doesn't get it she's suing me for full custody. Apparently she read in the society column that we'd gotten married and saw it as her opportunity for more money. I don't want her anywhere near Aimee, ever."

Trish was speechless as terror struck her heart.

"She can't have her. I won't allow it. What are you thinking of doing Davis? This is ridiculous, Aimee's never even met her. How does she plan on proving she's more qualified to parent her than you?"

"I know if I pay her she'll keep pulling this bullshit through the rest of Aimee's life, but I don't want to put Aimee through a custody battle. I don't know what to do." He pushed his hand through his hair.

"Even if she doesn't get custody she can push for visitation. I don't want Aimee exposed to anything that has to do with Jasmine."

"Can I make a suggestion? Maybe you should hire a private investigator to find out what she's been doing for the last four years. See if what she's been up to is something you shouldn't expose a child to. You need to line up your ammunition. I'll pay the money myself if she'll sign away her parental rights. I'd adopt Aimee in a second if I could." Trish was getting pissed now, and when that happened people scattered, because she meant business.

"That's a thought, about the investigator I mean. Yeah, the more I think about it the more I like it. She's the scum of the earth. Hell, she never even wanted Aimee in the first place. I had to pay her just to go through with the pregnancy. Bottom line is the money. Jasmine thinks having money is the most important thing in the world and she won't be happy until she's rich beyond her wildest dreams. Aimee is just a means to an end for her."

"Baby, I'm so sorry to have closed you out. I was afraid you'd freak out on me but I see now I've got my best friend on my side and Aimee has her real mommy on her side. We can't lose."

"Don't treat me like a fragile child Davis. This is a partnership we have here. For better or worse and when the worse comes that's when we need each other the most. I love you and Aimee and I'll do anything to keep you both safe. Now let's have some make-up sex." She kissed Davis deeply, sensuously with a touch of urgency behind it. She didn't have to ask twice, and thankfully it was Saturday so they had all day.

The week flew by for both Davis and Trish. Friday hit and they prepared to meet with the private detective Jake had recommended. They were meeting in Jake's office at the law firm and Trish was glad Jake was included in the meeting. The investigator's name was Tom Wilkins and he seemed to know his business well. He looked like just an average guy, someone who easily blended into a crowd. Davis supplied a picture of his ex-wife, Jasmine Sinclair, from her high school year book. Apparently Davis had destroyed any pictures he'd had of her a long time ago. Tom asked Davis a lot of questions about her personal habits and what she liked to do for fun. Davis told him everything he could, including how he paid her to keep the baby and what she did afterward. He was getting ready to leave when Trish suggested that their security company be aware of Tom so they didn't interfere accidentally with the investigation. After the ordeal with creepy they were pretty sensitive about people hanging around. When Trish opened the door to Jake's office she was surprised to see Duke holding his arms out to stop a woman from getting to the doors.

"Davis there's a woman Duke is trying to prevent from getting to this office, take a look and see if it's Jasmine." Davis and Tom both came to the door at the same time.

"Yeah, that's her all right. Now you have a better visual Tom. Good luck dealing with her, she's a bitch and a half."

When Davis turned to Trish she was white as a ghost. He started toward and she fainted into his arms. She woke up on Jake's couch with a rag on her forehead and Davis tapping her cheek. She could barely hear him with the ringing in her ears. Trish tried to sit up Davis held her back.

"Stay right where you are. Don't move, got it?"

127

Jake's secretary poked her head into the office and spoke to Davis.

"It's all set. He'll see her right now."

"Thanks Jane. Come on little lady, you're coming with me right now." Davis took Trish's hand and helped her stand up as he led her to the elevators.

"Where are we going Davis? Where did Tom and Duke go? How long was I out, I've never fainted before in my life."

"We're going up to the ninth floor to see Dr. McNeil. Jane and Melissa both see him, said he was good. You haven't been feeling good for too long now, it's time we get some answers. No arguments."

Davis did the paperwork in the exam room with Trish while they waited for the doctor to come in. Dr. McNeil was very nice. Trish and Davis both liked him. He examined Trish from top to bottom. He told Trish to get dressed and the nurse would take them to his office when she was done. Dr. McNeil had done some blood tests and urine tests before the exam and Trish and Davis waited nervously for him in his office, holding each other's hand for support.

Both of them jumped, startled by the door opening. Dr. McNeil took his seat behind the desk and looked over Trish's chart before he spoke.

"Well I have some of the preliminary test results which concur with what I found in my examination. Mr. & Mrs. Sinclair you're going to have a baby."

Dr. McNeil broke into a grin as he looked at the expressions on their faces. Total shock showed on both their faces. When Davis looked at Trish she began to cry, putting her hand over her mouth in disbelief.

"Wow. This is great! Baby, we made a baby, are you o.k. with this?"

Trish, too overcome to speak, smiled and shook her head yes as tears of joy ran down her face. Dr. McNeil gave them a few minutes before he started to speak again.

"Have you had any morning sickness Mrs. Sinclair?"

"Um, no, not really. I had one incident about a week ago of vomiting but that was in the afternoon and only that one time. Mostly it's been the tiredness and today's fainting episode. Other than that I feel fine."

"Well I'm going to tell you the same thing I tell all my patients, listen to your body. If you feel tired, lie down. If you're hungry, eat. Right now you're a little underweight so I would encourage you to eat more regularly and until the tiredness passes I think you should watch, possibly even cut, your working hours. Once you start on your vitamins your energy levels will gradually get better, but for now take it easy. Otherwise you have no limitations to speak of. We'll make an appointment for a re-check in about a month but in the meantime, if you have any questions, I want you to call me. No question is stupid. We have a packet of information for you at the front desk and a prescription for your vitamins. If the vitamins upset your stomach you can take them at bedtime or with your meals. Any questions?"

Trish and Davis nodded their heads as if they were bobble heads. "Great. If you'll follow me up front we'll get you all set and congratulations again." Dr. McNeil smiled as he shook Davis' hand and patted Trish on the back. Both Trish and Davis smiled widely until their faces began to hurt.

Duke escorted them back to Trish's office and shrugged his shoulders as Melissa gave him a 'what the hell's going on' look. Trish and Davis went into her office and closed the door, immediately hugging each other.

"I guess I'm pretty naïve about stuff like this cause I never saw it coming. I'm so happy I don't know where to put myself, and a little scared too. How about you Davis, how do you feel?"

"Glorious. Thrilled. Excited. Proud. You name a happy emotion and I'm all over it. I love you so much and I can't wait to enjoy watching your body change as you carry our little person inside you. There's nothing more sexy than my woman carrying my baby, and I can't wait to get you into bed." Davis plastered kisses all over Trish's face.

"Then we better get going home. Do you need to go back to your office before we go?"

"Yeah, I'll be back in a few minutes. Do you mind if I tell Jake and Larry the news?"

"Please feel free to tell anyone you want except Melissa and Duke, I get to tell them." Trish rubbed her hands together in anticipation.

"You got it." Davis broke into a quick jog back to his office.

"Melissa and Duke, could you please come in here for a minute?" They both came in and sat down as quickly as humanly possible without tripping over each other.

"Everything's alright, Dr. McNeil did a complete exam and some tests and as it turns out It's just a little case of pregnancy." Trish laughed out loud at the look on Melissa's face.

"Yes! I'm so happy for you. You are happy aren't you cause if you're not I'm going to have to slap you silly." Melissa threatened.

"Thrilled. Both of us. I should have guessed but honestly it never entered my mind. Now I feel kind of stupid, but in a happy way, of course." Trish qualified.

"How far along are you?" Duke asked.

"Ummmm, really good question. I'm pretty sure I'm two months along, I think. Dr. McNeil will be able to tell more when the blood results come back. I guess I should call and check on that tomorrow. Gee Duke you're mighty handy to have around. How do you feel about changing diapers?"

"I don't do windows or diapers." He said dryly.

"Ditto here." Melissa piped in.

"Gosh, I still can't get over it. My face is starting to hurt from smiling so much."

"Congratulations, daddy." Melissa gave Davis a hug.

"Yeah, good news travel fast. Congrats." Duke shook Davis' hand.

"Thanks guys. You two are in charge of her when I'm not around. Make sure she eats and if she looks tired make her lay down for a while. Doctor's orders. Husband's orders too."

"Yes sir." They replied in unison as they saluted Davis.

"Ready baby?" Davis took her hand and kissed it before he led her out the door. Duke followed, back in security mode now.

Chapter 26

Trish and Davis' wedding day number two, as they liked to refer to it, dawned beautifully. The weather was unseasonably warm without a hint of humidity. The sun was shining brilliantly on the fresh, bright green's of spring along with the watercolor pastels of early flowers blooming. Even the air smelled fresh, the light breeze of spring carrying along the sweet scent of spring flowers and blooming cherry trees that looked as glorious as they smelled, with a riot of pink and white petals clinging to the invisible branches of the tree. Morning dew clung to everything in sight. The bright sunlight hit the precious drops making them sparkle and shimmer with tiny rainbow effects.

It looked and felt magically enchanted as the birds busily built their nests in anticipation of the young they would raise within the sturdy walls. The wonders of nature, Trish thought, as she opened the French doors leading out to the patio, her coffee in hand she walked out to sit at the table and watch the day unfold. As soon as she sat down Davis swooped in behind her silently and took her coffee away from her, replacing it with decaf and a glass of orange juice before he sat down. When she saw him sitting there with her old cup of coffee she was shocked that he had been able to sneak-up on her without her realizing it.

"Okay, what are you up to Mr. Sneaky. You've got a rather smug look on your face and I don't trust it."

"The baby wanted a glass of orange juice and decaf coffee so I got it for him."

"Really? When did the baby tell you this? I didn't hear a thing and who said it's a he and not a she?"

"He did."

"How long have you been talking to the baby Davis? Do I need to call you a different kind of doctor? Maybe take you to a *'special' hospital*?" Trish was laughing now.

"A father and son have a special bond, we just know these things. Sort of like a women's intuition only reversed. Doctor's don't write about it because you women get jealous, but it happens every day." Davis stated this as absolute fact.

"Well we'll just have to wait and see won't we. Oh, by the way, that was decaf coffee I was drinking so if you need your jolt you'll have to talk Josie into making you your own pot."

"See, another reason we need another man around the house, too many female hormones flying around this house and you all stick together."

"I thought you liked being around flying female hormones."

"Wouldn't have it any other way." Davis leaned over and kissed Trish gently on the lips.

"When do you think we should tell Aimee about the baby?"

"Tonight at the reception, maybe we could let her make the announcement after the ceremony. What do you think about that idea?"

"That's fine with me as long as you remember that once you give a microphone to a four year-old girl you may never get it back."

"We'll cut the sound if it goes too long but I think she'd love it."

"I agree. We'll do it that way then." Trish hoped Aimee would be as happy to tell everyone as Trish and Davis had been.

"Well speaking of Aimee, look who's here!" Davis opened his arms and beckoned her to come sit on his lap. She was still groggy with sleep and her long hair hung in a riot of tangles around her face while she rested her head on his chest.

"Morning big girl, how did you sleep? Did you have happy dreams?" Trish asked. Aimee just nodded her head sleepily. The three of them sat there on the patio enjoying the sounds and smells of nature until Josie surprised them all and brought breakfast out to them on the patio.

"Josie thank you so much! What a great idea to have breakfast out here, I don't know what we'd do without you." Trish loved Josie and considered her family.

"Come and join us Josie the weathers beautiful." Trish and Davis both extended their arms in invitation to Josie as she hesitated slightly.

"You're family Josie and you always will be. Sit." Davis commanded. He'd been doing that a lot lately Trish thought with a smile.

At least Josie suppressed the urge to salute.

Before Trish knew it she was swept into motion by Melissa and Sylvia as all the girls, including Aimee, had hair and nail appointments together. She would have preferred to stay on the patio all day but when she saw the look of excitement on Sylvia and Aimee's faces she found herself joining in the feeling of euphoria.

Trish and Aimee wore their street clothes to the hall and decided to get dressed there. As they entered the banquet room they both made sounds of delight and awe as they took in the beauty and splendor of the room. Flowers were abundant in a variety of pastels with baby's breath, creating a feeling of little white clouds throughout the arrangements. The centerpieces on the tables matched the arrangements by the altar with the exception of the tea lights glowing throughout the arrangements. The top tablecloths were also done in a rainbow of pastels throughout the room. The room was so elegant it made Trish feel like a fairy princess. Aimee was so speechless she just stood there in the doorway with her mouth gaping open. Instead of the dance floor being in the center of the room it was at the far end of the room opposite the bridal party's banquet table.

For the ceremony an arbor stood adorned with pastel flowers in a vine formation that trailed to the floor. From the center of the arbor to the middle of the banquet room there was a ribbon of satin lying on the floor, marking the way for Aimee to spread her pastel rose petals as she walked up to the arbor. Now Trish was glad they had hired a photographer because this was certainly something she would want to show her clients when planning a wedding. It was perfect elegance without being over the top, and it had all been Sylvia's vision. The lady had class, that was for sure.

Trish took Aimee's hand and led her to the changing room as she heard cars beginning to pull up to the front doors of the banquet hall. Trish was thankful Josie was there to help Aimee get dressed. Trish's dress was made of a pearlescent satin in a barely blue color that gave a slight rainbow effect when the light reflected off the fabric. The cut was umpire with a slightly fitted skirt that clung in all the right places. The back was cut down to the middle of Trish's back. The neckline was a low cut cowl made entirely of imported irish lace, dyed to match the satin of the dress, with tiny seed pearls strewn throughout the lace in a very delicate and feminine effect. Her shoes were dyed to match the dress with a medium heel in a pump style with matching seed pearls around the opening of the shoes. Trish had refused to remove the plain, thin gold band she wore from the first ceremony at the hospital. She would forever consider that to be her true wedding ring. She had gotten Davis a plain gold thick band and had their names and wedding date engraved inside which she planned to give him today since he had no band from the first wedding. She slid his wedding ring onto her thumb so she wouldn't forget it. In her ears she wore a pair of simple pearl stud earrings. She wore her hair down in large spiral curls and had a fresh flower headpiece in a wreath style accented with baby's breath and the flowers echoing the pastels of the rest of the flowers throughout the banquet hall. Melissa's dress was a mirror image of Trish's but in a barely there pink and Aimee's did the same in light lavender.

When Sylvia walked into the room the sight of all three of them standing together took her breath away, they were simply stunning.
"I have never in my life seen such a portrait of elegance and beauty in my whole life. You ladies are breathtakingly beautiful and Aimee I swear to God you look just like a fairy princess." Aimee giggled like she had played a joke on Sylvia.
"Well it's time to get started, are you all ready?" Sylvia asked.

Jake walked into the room so he could escort Trish down the isle. He stopped suddenly with his mouth gaping open as he took in the sight of her. He was so proud of Trish and Davis but when he saw how elegant she looked he was stunned into silence. Unable to speak he simply extended his arm for Trish to take and patted her hand as she rested it in the crook of his arm.
"I hope Davis will be able to speak his vows because you have left me nearly speechless my dear, your beauty is second to none." Jake said as they began to walk down the satin runner.

Trish looked up and saw Davis and Larry standing next to the pastor in their traditional black tuxedos. Davis looked so handsome in his tux, his boutonniere matching Trish's headpiece and bouquet she carried. They smiled to each other as Trish walked down the isle with Melissa and Aimee standing up across from Davis. For the first time in her life Trish felt like a princess. Jake took her hand and handed it to Davis. They took

their vows again, this time in front of two hundred of Sylvia and Jake's closest friends.
Trish had expected Davis to just pretend to slide a ring on her finger when that part of the ceremony came but instead was surprised to see him with another ring for this ceremony. As she looked at her new ring tears sprang to he eyes. Davis had gotten her a band ring with four marquis cut gemstones, between each marquis was a round diamond. It looked just like the flowers for the ceremony with the four marquis being a pink sapphire, blue topaz, champagne diamond, and peridot.
"It's so beautiful." Tears filled Trish's eyes and Melissa jammed a tissue into her free hand.

 When the ceremony was concluded the pastor introduced the new couple as Mr. & Mrs. Davis Sinclair and Miss Aimee Sinclair as the crowd applauded. When the applause died down Davis took the microphone and asked everyone for their attention.

"Well, I'm the luckiest man in the world today. Look at these two, they're the two most beautiful women in the world and I'm the lucky man who gets to share my life with them. Aimee, Trish and I wanted to get you something to help you remember today but we knew you don't care too much for jewelry. So we thought, what would Aimee like? Then it dawned on us what you like the most in the whole wide world, so here comes Duke with your wedding present."

As Aimee looked up Duke approached her with a puppy in his arms, a very, very large puppy.

"Aimee this puppy is called an Irish Wolfhound and his name is Zeus. What do you think? Do you like him?" But Aimee wasn't listening as she already had her arms around the puppy's neck as Duke bent down to let her see him better.

"I think that's a yes folks. Thank you for sharing our joy with us today." Davis replaced the microphone into the stand and took Trish's hand as they all gathered around Zeus.

After fussing with Zeus for a while Trish had Duke take him back to his kennel while she took Aimee to the bathroom with Melissa. Trish couldn't stop staring at her new wedding ring thinking she couldn't have picked a better one herself. As she was showing Melissa her ring there was shouting outside the bathroom doors in the hallway. Trish and Melissa looked at each other suspiciously, knowing something was very wrong. Melissa told Trish to keep Aimee in the restroom until she came back. A few minutes later she was back with Sylvia and Josie following close behind her.

"What's going on out there?" Trish asked while she helped Aimee dry her hands.

"Well, Josie and Duke are taking Aimee home so she can have some fun with Zeus before she has to go to bed. Would you like that Aimee?" Sylvia asked in an excited way.

"Yea! Wight now?"

"Yep. Dukes all ready. He has Zeus in the car waiting so lets go with Josie and Duke right now and I'll see you tomorrow, okay?" Sylvia kissed her goodbye as did Melissa and Trish. When they were gone out of ear shot Trish squared onto both of them, waiting for the bad news.

"Somehow, Jasmine found out about the wedding. She came storming in yelling and demanding that she wanted to see her daughter right now. That you and Davis had no right to keep her from her own flesh and blood. Luckily Duke intercepted her in the foyer before she made it into the actual dining area. Davis came out to try to talk to her. He seems to have calmed her down some and now he's trying to convince her to leave, and if that doesn't work they'll have to call the police. She sounds more than a little drunk and she reeks of liquor."

"Davis would like you to stay in here until he can get her out. He's afraid she'll go crazy again if she sees you."

"I'm so, so sorry this happened tonight Sylvia. If we had any idea she would have done this we would have taken more precautions. How much do you think the other guests know?"

"It's certainly not your fault honey, how could you have known. I don't think too much damage was done thanks to Duke. He's pretty sharp to have caught her before she got into the dining room. I'm quite sure she never even got a glimpse of Aimee, so that's good." As Sylvia finished they heard a knock on the door while Davis pushed it open.

"All clear ladies. She's gone. I packed her off in a cab."

Trish grabbed Davis' arm in an effort to steady herself while the room began to spin. Davis grabbed her and sat her down on the chair in the lounge area as he pushed her head down to her knees. He knelt down next to her as he stroked her back and told her to breathe. The look of confusion on Sylvia's face was clear.

Melissa decided to help out a little "She's alright Sylvia, she's pregnant and having a little dizzy spell. She'll be fine in a minute, I'll go get her some water."

"You're having a baby? Oh my God that's wonderful! I'm so happy for you. Why didn't you tell me sooner?"

"We had planned on having Aimee make the announcement after dinner. She doesn't know yet either. Now that won't be happening. Are you feeling any better, baby?" Davis asked as he kissed Trish's forehead.

"Yeah, I'm fine now. I just had a thought, maybe Sylvia would you like to make the baby announcement tonight? You'd really be doing us a favor, not that we don't already owe you enough." Trish's color began to come back to her face.

"You would seriously let me do that? I'd be honored."

"Great. All settled then. Let's go eat." Davis said cheerfully, as if he didn't have a care in the world. Trish knew better but let it go, struggling to get back into a festive mood.

The rest of the evening went well as people began to dance and socialize after dinner. When it was time for Davis and Trish to dance their wedding dance Sylvia announced the pregnancy and the audience applauded. Sylvia made a point of the fact that they were already married when the baby was conceived to stop any gossip. Trish was glad Sylvia was having such a good time at her own party. She had never seen Sylvia so comfortable in a situation as she was tonight. She was in her element and loving every minute of it.

Trish was glad they had decided not to do the chicken dance at this wedding because she was just too tired. Davis stared lovingly into Trish's eyes as the slow danced together.

"What's your body telling you Trish?" She wiggled her eyebrows vigorously and smiled.

"I think it's telling you that you're tired and need to get off your feet and get some sleep."

"Some of that is accurate. I am tired and I would like to get off my feet and eventually I could use some sleep, but I had something else in mind before the sleep part. You know how horny pregnant women can be." She smiled as she kissed his lips and then took the kiss even deeper when she thrust her tongue into his surprised mouth.

"Ever do it in the back of a limo Sinclair?" Trish asked playfully.

"God I love you. Let's get the hell out of here."

As it turned out it was a good thing they did it in the back of the limo because by the time they reached the house Trish was sound asleep in Davis' arms. Davis carried Trish to bed and took off her headpiece, gown, shoes and stockings and tucked her neatly into bed. He checked in on Aimee only to find her sound asleep on the edge of her bed because Zeus took up most of the bed and the entire pillow. When Davis went into the family room he saw Duke sitting on the couch reading a book.

"Hey Duke thanks a lot for tonight. Would you like to have a drink with me to celebrate the wedding. I feel like you got the short end of the stick having to leave so early."

"Sure. I'd love one and don't worry about tonight I'm not much on partying anyway. I'm sure I had a lot more fun with Josie, Aimee and Zeus than you had at the party."

"Yeah. I saw Zeus in Aimee's bed when I checked on her."

"That damn dog loves that little girl so much Josie and I couldn't keep the two of them apart. When Josie put Aimee to bed that dog laid outside her door and cried worse than a baby until we finally let him in with her. Then he fell right to sleep."

"Did Romeo and Zeus meet yet?" Davis asked.

"They looked at each other from a distance but didn't care enough to check each other out. Romeo laid on the bookshelf and watched Aimee and Zeus play and that's about it. I think they'll be cool together."

When Trish woke up in the middle of the night she didn't remember how she got there or who undressed her but she had a good idea. Davis wasn't in bed so she put on her silk short robe and started looking for him. She checked in Aimee's room and saw Zeus and Aimee sleeping peacefully in her bed. When she got to the family room she saw Davis sprawled on the couch, still dressed in his tux although he had taken the tie and the cumber bun off. She went and kneeled next to him and began to gently unbutton his shirt as she kissed her way down his chest. When she reached his pants she undid them and continued her kissing trail. Davis woke when Trish had taken his erection into her mouth. She began to lave her tongue over it's tip while she cupped his balls in her other hand. Davis reached down and put his hand in her hair as she continued her assault on his increasingly hardening erection. She moaned in pleasure as she took all of him into her mouth and sucked deeply over and over. Davis' body broke out in a sweat. When he was fully erect and near completion Trish undid her robe and mounted him as she bucked fast and furiously until they both shuttered together with their mutual climax. Exhausted, Trish laid on top of Davis as she recovered her breath. She gazed lovingly into his eyes.

"Hi. I missed you in bed so I came and found you."

"Thank goodness you found me."

"I say that every day since we've been together. Come to bed and I'll finish undressing you there." Trish took his hand and led him to the bedroom, keeping her promise.

Sunday afternoon Sylvia and Jake came over for a picnic style lunch at Davis and Trish's house. They sat on the patio and watched as Aimee and Zeus romped around in the backyard. Aimee giggled every time Zeus licked her face and ran around while Zeus barked and chased her. Poor Zeus was so clumsy he tripped more than he ran, trying to get his legs to coordinate themselves with his brain.

When the talk turned to more serious subjects Trish brought up the Jasmine incident.

"Davis, I've been wondering about this all day. I know we were told that creepy guy acted alone but now I wonder if that's right. How would Jasmine know so much about us without the help of someone else? I mean, is it possible that when the kidnapping didn't pay-off and creepy was killed she had to come up with another way to get the money? Don't you think the timing is a little odd? Someone must have told her I have money or she wouldn't bother. What do you think?"

"I never thought about it that way but I can see your point. I think it's something worth mentioning to Tom and have him check it out. Very interesting theory. You're one smart cookie, cookie. Jake what do you think?"

"I agree. I never put the two together but now that she mentions it the odds of both those things happening within a four or five month span are pretty long at that. I have to talk to Tom about another matter tomorrow so I'll mention it to him and let you know his impressions."

Davis caught Trish stifling a yawn and with that took her hand and pulled her gently out of her chair.

"Excuse us for a minute. My wife needs to lay down for a little while. I'll just get her settled into bed and then I'll be back." Trish began to protest but one look at Davis' face told her she wasn't going to win this one because he was right, she was tired and did need a nap. She followed obediently as Davis led the way.

When Trish woke up three hours later she found Aimee, Davis and Zeus all asleep in bed with her, strewn every which way across the king size bed. She laid there a long time enjoying the peace and quiet of their slumber, watching their facial expressions. Zeus was running somewhere in his dreams as all four of his feet moved at the same time for once. Trish finally slid off the bed and went into the kitchen to make dinner, knowing that when they woke up they'd be hungry as bears. While the casserole baked in the oven Trish went into the family room to read more of the information the doctor had given her. Romeo crawled into her lap as she went through the brochures and coupons one by one until she felt she had a good grasp of the information. Trish wanted to learn as much as she could about pregnancy and childbirth so once she finished the brochures she moved over to the computer. She was just starting to get some pictures of fetus' when Davis came up behind her and started to rub her back and neck.

"What's up?"

"That's a picture of our baby's development up to two months. Isn't it a miracle. How could anyone purposely kill something so blessed and miraculous? How can they argue that this isn't life? I can't wait until we have an ultrasound of our baby to show everyone. What was Aimee's pregnancy like for you. Did Jasmine include you in it?"

"No. Jasmine didn't include me in it. She tried to ignore it herself and she was pretty successful until the labor started."

"So then you don't mind if I'm a little obsessive about the baby. I don't want you to get bored or mad at me if you've already been there done that kind of thing." Trish worried her lip as she thought about what was ahead.

"Please don't ever think that I don't want to participate. I plan on being at every doctor's appointment and every ultrasound with you. Just try getting rid of me now, you did marry me twice you know."

Trish turned off the computer just as Aimee and Zeus came running in. Davis and Trish ran to catch Zeus and take him outside before he had an accident in the house. Davis won the race for the dog so Trish went into the kitchen to check dinner. When she looked out the window she saw a woman standing on the sidewalk across the street looking into their yard while Davis and Aimee tried to catch Zeus. Trish got a sinking feeling of dread as she saw the security guard approach her. She couldn't hear what the woman was saying but she could tell from the gestures she was making that she wasn't happy. The woman eventually moved down the sidewalk as the guard stood his ground and watched until she was out of sight. When Davis and Aimee came back in the house Trish sent Aimee to set the table in the dining room so she could talk to Davis.

"Did you see the woman the security guard was talking to on the sidewalk just now? Was that Jasmine?"

"Yeah, that was her. I pretended I didn't notice anything so Aimee would ignore it too. We need to do something so we can have more privacy. Something to keep her away from us. Somehow she has all our information."

"I think maybe we should have a security company come out and go over the property with a fine tooth comb and tell us what they would suggest. I don't even know what's available on the market for security other than an alarm system. Do you think you could take some time off if I can get an appointment sometime this week? I'd like to be here for the meeting too."

"You're right. I was hoping her poison wouldn't touch us here but obviously that's not happening so we need to do something else, fast."

"Do you think we should maybe have Josie and Aimee stay with Sylvia and Jake for a while or maybe just during the day until you get home."

"I don't think that would do any good. Jasmine knows where they live and once she figured out they weren't here that's the next place she'd look."

"Well I'll call a couple security companies first thing in the morning and we can go from there. Maybe we should tell Anna

Wells at the preschool what's going on just in case, we need to update her information anyway. I need to be added to the pick-up list along with Duke and maybe even Melissa and Larry too. You need to do that though, they won't take my word for it since I'm not her biological mother. I wish I were her mother."

"I know baby, I wish you were too. Maybe when this is all over we can work something out like maybe you adopting her."

"You'd consider letting me do that?" Tears welled up in Trish's eyes as she thought about the happiness she would feel to make Aimee hers.

"God, I've got to get these hormones under control, I feel like all I do is cry lately. Seriously, I'm honored you would even consider it."

"You are so fucking sexy I can't stand it."

"Remember that in about six months sailor and I'll show you a good time you won't forget."

Chapter 27

Trish and Davis met with three different security companies during the course of the week and had asked Duke to sit in on the meetings for his opinion as well. They decided on the deluxe interior and exterior package, which included alarm systems, fencing system, live exterior patrols, and personal bodyguards. Jake had made arrangements for all the law offices as well as Celebrations to be swept for bugging devices. Everyone was stunned when about ten devices were found throughout the law offices but what really surprised everyone was that some were found in Celebrations as well. Three in all were there in Trish's office, Melissa's phone and attached to the back of the coffee pot in the conference room. Someone was spending a lot of time and money to keep track of the Sinclair family and they needed to find out who.

As the weeks went by the security tightened. Trish and Davis felt their privacy invaded and their nerves fraying. There were at least three sightings of Jasmine each week while Tom continued to dig into her past. She still hadn't made any more overt moves, just stood watching from a distance and being careful to not break any laws. Nothing could be done but wait for her to make her next move. One day when Trish went into the kitchen to get a drink of water she screamed loudly when she looked out the window at a man's face peering in at her from outside, his nose almost touching the glass. He was their security and he had almost given her a heart attack. Trish finally snapped and called Davis hysterically crying.

"Davis please can we go away for a while, anywhere." Davis felt helpless as Trish sobbed on the phone to him while she trembled uncontrollably. She was breathing heavy and gasping.

"Is Josie there honey. Let me talk to Josie."

"She e e 's no o o t h ee re." She managed to get out.

"I'm coming home right now Trish. Listen to me. Go lay down on the couch in the family room and turn on the television. Can you do that for me? Take some deep breaths right now while

143

you go into the family room. Come on I can't hear your deep breaths Trish. Are you to the couch yet?" Davis spoke to Trish as he packed his briefcase and ran out the door.

"Yeeessss." She was starting to sound a little better.

"Good baby now lie down. Make sure your feet are up and keep taking the deep breaths for me. I'm already on my way. Just stay on the phone with me while I drive home."

"No! Don't drive while you talk on the phone, it's dangerous. I'm a lot better now, really, I promise. I'll stay right here on the couch until you get home. I'm hanging up now." And she did exactly what she promised.

When Davis ran into the house he found Trish lying on the couch and deep breathing. On his way home he had called Dr. McNeil for some advice about acceptable ways to calm Trish down without drugs. The doctor wasn't happy that Trish was under this kind of stress while being pregnant and thought going out of town for a while might be a good idea, and Davis had to agree with that himself. He would talk to Trish and decide where they should go, someplace peaceful.

Once Davis reassured himself that Trish was all right he told her about his conversation with Dr. McNeil.

"So where do you think you'd like to go?"

"I have no idea. I've never been anyplace but the convent and Harbor Springs, I don't think the trip to Boston counts because I was blindfolded for that one." She tried to lighten the mood a bit. She was feeling very guilty now about making Davis come home from work and her freaking out.

"Someplace quiet and calm and relaxing. Is there such a place?"

"Wait, I just had an idea. Jake and Sylvia have a house on one of the islands of Hawaii, almost a private island really. Do you think you'd like to spend some time there? If we got bored we could always go to one of the bigger islands for a day trip. You know we never did get to have a honeymoon."

"That sounds absolutely perfect, do you think they would let us use it. I'm willing to pay anything they ask, really."

"Great. I'll call Aunt Sylvia right now. You stay put." Davis pointed his finger at her in a gesture of authority.

"Yes, sir."

Davis went into their home office and Trish didn't see him again for another hour. When he came out he was energized and excited. He hadn't been on a vacation since Aimee was born and it was high time to remedy that.

"Okay we are all set. Sylvia gave us the go ahead on Hawaii, in fact she's coming to stay here for the week we're gone to help with Aimee and Zeus and, well, it's just easier for her to come here. Duke has agreed to spend the week with us but don't worry, there's a guest house on the property that he can stay at and he won't come up to the main house unless he's called. Sylvia assures me he can't even see the main house from the guest house. Sylvia wanted to know if we wanted any domestic help and I went out on a limb and said no, hope that's alright with you. I told her to have the staff stock the kitchen, clean the house and take off for a week. Private jet is ready to go, we just have to tell them when we're leaving. Did I forget anything?"

"You're wonderful. I just have to grab my toothbrush and I'm ready!"

"What about clothes?"

"I don't think I'll need anything more than a light robe, if you understand my meaning." She smiled her sexy, smoldering look.

"I see. Well I guess you're right, after all it is our honeymoon." He moved toward Trish like a prowling tiger about to attack and, as she giggled wildly, he pounced.

Within two hours they were on the plane to Hawaii. Trish felt an incredible sense of freedom. She had never been on a vacation in her life so she had no preconceived ideas about it. Davis liked the idea that he was the one taking her for the first time, she was a vacation virgin he teased her and he assured her he would show her a 'good time'.

"Of course you will, you always do."

The house was absolutely perfect. It was open and airy with three bedrooms and four baths. The color scheme was the same throughout the whole house with its varying shades of blues highlighted differently in each room. Lovely teak wood warmed all the rooms and it had hardwood floors throughout. The showers and footed bathtubs were big enough for two with beautiful scenes depicted in mosaic tiles, each one displaying a different underwater scene. It gave you the feeling of snorkeling as you laid back and relaxed. The kitchen was a galley style, not overly big but fully functional. Trish and Davis took turns cooking and vowed to keep it simple. Another thing Trish liked about the house, beside the spectacular ocean view, was that it was a ranch style so if you had guests staying with you the layout allowed you complete privacy from each other. Each bedroom had a set of French doors that led out to a private patio and a small kitchenette for morning coffee and a light breakfast. They also had a built-in pool that looked out over the ocean, giving you the feeling that you were actually in the ocean when you swam in it. Trish had never lived in such luxury but she was sure she could get used to it.

While they were there they lived their lives exactly as they pleased for the whole week. They walked around most of the time nude, both indoors and outdoors. They ate when they were hungry, napped when they were tired and made love anywhere and anytime they felt like it. They read books they'd been meaning to read, took leisurely walks along the shore, skinny dipped when the sun became too much and caught up on movies they had meant to see but had never gotten a chance to. Most importantly they reconnected and talked about anything and everything. They decided that they needed a date night once a week to stay connected to each other, and they also agreed that Sunday's would still be Aimee day for all three of them. One thing they agreed on immediately was that they had to enroll Zeus in an obedience class that all three of them would attend. He wasn't getting any smaller and they needed him to listen before Trish's pregnancy got so far along she wouldn't be able to chase and discipline him, plus it was good family time, which was an added bonus.

A habit that Davis had gotten into every morning and every evening was kissing their unborn baby good morning and good night. He would kiss her belly and carry on a conversation as if he could hear the replies of the baby. Sometimes Trish felt like she was intruding on a private conversation.

"Did you two need me to leave you alone for a few minutes?" Trish would ask as she laughed at Davis' antics.

"No that's okay we don't have any secrets from you." As seriously as possible.

Trish hadn't realized how much bigger her stomach had gotten until she had to put on her clothes for the trip home. She was stunned when she needed a rubber band to close her pants and she couldn't zip them all the way. She borrowed one of Davis' t-shirts to cover her bulging tummy. Trish was rather appalled at how quickly it happened, but Davis found it very sexy. He would rub his hand over her and kiss her senseless. If Davis could have carried the baby for Trish he would have.

While their plane was being refueled Trish and Davis raided the gift shops at the airport and bought presents for everyone. Trish had never had so much fun shopping in her life, Davis kept her in stitches the entire time. On one hand Trish hated to go home but on the other hand she missed Aimee, and even the craziness of Zeus, and felt much better equipped to handle the stress that they were going through. Once she pulled away she saw that eventually this trouble would pass and that realization helped keep things in perspective and deal with the invasion of privacy she felt in her own home.

Trish and Davis fell back into the same routine easily, feeling rested and revitalized. Melissa had held down the fort at Celebrations quite admirably and as a reward she and Davis decided to make arrangements with Sylvia to rent the Hawaii home for a week for Melissa and Larry to enjoy. They made the private jet available to them and happily sent them on their way two weeks after she and Davis had returned. Trish had hired a temporary employee to take over Melissa's duties for the week. She had also made an appointment with Jake to give forty percent of the company to Melissa. She had more than earned it and she knew the business just as well as Trish, but most important she trusted Melissa completely. Trish could only say that about a handful of people and counted Melissa as her best friend. She admired the way Melissa told it like it was even if she knew it didn't agree with Trish's opinion. She didn't invite conflict but she didn't run from it either and that was important when dealing with a bridezilla on a ranting fit over something trivial and easily fixed.

Trish and Melissa would have their hands full training new employees throughout the summer if they wanted them up and running independently by the holidays. With the baby being due in December they wouldn't be able to count on Trish to attend any events, or even make it into the office at all. Trish hadn't told Melissa any of her plans because she wanted to surprise her. This new position in the company would more than triple Melissa's salary and give her a sense of ownership. She had worked her ass off to get here. Davis was all for the plan, surprised that Trish had even mentioned staying home with the baby for a while until she was done nesting and bonding with him. By the time Trish gave birth to the baby Aimee would be in kindergarten so Josie would be able to help her more. If it got too crazy Trish even considered opening a daycare center adjoining Celebrations and having Josie and her sister Helen run it. But now Trish was getting ahead of herself, right now the focus was on securing Celebrations future. Jake had the papers drawn up and now they just had to wait until Melissa and Larry got back.

Right now Trish needed to focus on the baby, today they had an appointment for their first ultrasound and Trish thought she'd float away with all the water they make you drink beforehand. As the technician settled Trish and Davis into the exam room she spoke non-stop, knowing they were nervous and excited. She put the warmed gel on Trish's abdomen and smoothly glided the apparatus over Trish's belly. She suddenly stopped talking and turned the monitor away from Trish and Davis towards herself. Trish felt the slow rush of fear as she squeezed Davis' hand in concern. Davis looked at Trish and just shrugged his shoulders in an '*I don't know*' gesture. The technician quickly excused herself as she mumbled some lame reason for leaving.
"I'm scared Davis. I don't like the look on her face, like she was worried or confused. She does this all day, I would hope she knows what she's doing."
"It'll be fine. Now don't go off with your imagination running wild. Patience, my love. We'll know soon enough." He heard the doctor's voice approaching their treatment room. The doctor seemed relaxed as he entered the room, all smiles and cheer. He picked up the device the technician had used and rolled it over Trish's belly as he squinted at the monitor.
"Let's print that image. This one too." Dr. McNeil instructed the technician as he continued to ignore Trish and Davis but was far more serious now.
"What's wrong?"
"Absolutely nothing is wrong." Dr. McNeil squeezed Trish's hand reassuringly.
"Then why did you have to come in and check things?"
"The technician has just never seen this particular situation before and she wanted me to double check her work. She's not allowed to discuss the test results with you so she asked me to come in and talk to you." He paused trying to collect his thoughts before he spoke again.

"Mr. and Mrs. Sinclair there's just no easy way to say this so I'm just going to blurt it out. You're having triplets. There are three fetus' and three very strong heartbeats, everything looks really good and they all seem to be healthy. For now, whatever you're doing keep going, it's working beautifully. We will be keeping a closer watch on you now that we know there's three of them in there. Make an appointment in two weeks and we'll start from there. Any questions?" Dr. McNeil smiled as he looked into two stunned faces. All they could both manage was a shake of their heads in response. Dr. McNeil left the office chuckling to himself. *Some days this job was really, really great.*

Trish and Davis went back to their offices never speaking to each other the whole time, each absorbed in their own thoughts. Three Babies! Kept streaming through Trish's mind over and over again. She walked past Duke and the temp without saying a word. She closed the door to her office and laid down on the daybed. She tried to examine her feelings but then suddenly realized that it really didn't matter how she felt because it was happening. Pure joy and awe overtook her. She suddenly realized that they never even thought to ask about the sexes. . *So God really does have a sense of humor.*
When Davis came to Trish's office to take them home for the day he looked at her while she broke into a huge grin. "We're having triplets and I think it's the best present I've ever gotten. I'm thrilled baby."
"Oh thank God you feel the same way I do." Trish kissed Davis several times before taking his hand and leading him out the door. Trish laughed out loud suddenly.
"What?"
"Poor Anna Wells is really going to get an ear full from Aimee tomorrow at preschool." Now they were both laughing like idiots all the way down in the elevator as the other occupants stared at them and took a few steps away. Even Duke eyed them warily.
"Relax Duke we haven't lost our minds yet. Found out today we're having triplets." Davis said as he addressed the whole elevator full of people and watched them all visibly relax. Everyone congratulated them as they exited the elevator.

CELEBRATION OF LIFE

The discussion with Aimee over dinner was interesting, to say the least, Davis tried to explain in four year-old terms how three babies could be in Trish's belly at the same time. They ended up deciding that the how didn't matter as much as the fact that she was going to be a big sister to three little babies, and of course the most important helper on the planet. Trish made sure she asked Aimee's opinion on as many things as possible so she felt involved. When they finished tucking Aimee in for the night they waited until they got into the family room before they burst out laughing. One thing was for sure Aimee didn't miss a trick and asked questions all night long. Just when they thought everything was settled she'd pop up with another question. Parenting could be mentally exhausting as well as physically. As they laid in bed, Davis started to lecture Trish's belly.

"Okay boys we need to have a meeting and set some ground rules. No kicking mommy in the kidney's. No fist fighting in the womb, it's too crowded in there to get any leverage anyway. Keep the pushing and shoving to a minimum. Got it? Good, now go to sleep and dream happy dreams." Davis kissed her belly three times, one for each baby, while Trish laughed hysterically.

"So now it's three boys is it? You're going to have a lot of apologizing to do if this boy theory of yours doesn't pan out."

"It's not theory, it's fact. Deal with it babe."

"We'll see about that."

Chapter 28

The meeting with the private investigator had both Trish and Davis on edge as they sat in Jake's office waiting for Tom to join them. Trish prayed for a miracle, sure she had used up all of her miracles with the triplets but was still hoping for one more. She grabbed Davis' hand and held it in a death grip until she saw him wince in pain.

"Get used to it buddy, I hear childbirth is hell on a man's hands."

Tom entered the office briskly with a thick file in his hands and took a seat, setting the file on the coffee table.

"Well overall I'd say it's good news for our side. Jasmine has an outstanding warrant for her arrest in New Mexico for human trafficking. Apparently she has had two other children since Aimee and allegedly sold both of them on the black market, although I don't have access to all the evidence in the case. I talked to the investigating officers and when I told them your situation they were much more forthcoming with information, off the record of course. Right now she's staying here in Harbor Springs at the Best Western and keeping a very low profile. Although there was one incident where she got drunk in the bar across from the hotel and told anybody who would listen that she was coming into some big money soon." Tom slid his hand over his face as he took a big breath before continuing.

"I'm still looking into any connection between Jasmine and Sean Murdock but my gut's telling me there's something there. They were both in New Mexico at the same time but that doesn't prove anything, yet that is. We're still looking into it. Now here's the bad news. Jasmine has gone to Child Services and requested visitation with Aimee. She's been assigned a court appointed attorney, a Mike Griffiths, who's already met with a very teary Jasmine playing the concerned mother role. She gave him the old people with money shindig and how, just because she's poor doesn't mean she doesn't have a right to see her darling baby girl. I almost lost my lunch when I heard that one. Still, she's pushing for a hearing and I suspect within the next week or two you'll be getting a visit from Child Services to start a home study."

"How can she get a judge to agree with her when she has an outstanding warrant for her arrest?" Trish asked.

"Judge doesn't know she has an outstanding warrant and even if she does have the warrant she's innocent until proven guilty, it's the law." Tom answered.

"So what can we do?" Trish was getting worried and she put a hand to her now very swollen belly.

"Right now you need to cooperate with Child Services and play the game. Don't trash Jasmine to anyone, it will make you look better in the end. I know it goes against your nature right now but this is really important to appear to be completely cooperative. Next, find a really good child custody lawyer, someone older who's been around awhile and has a good reputation with the courts. Someone who's experienced has a better chance of getting negative evidence admitted into the court records. For now that's all we can do. I'll keep digging on my end and you need to contact that attorney and get moving on that."

Trish and Davis left the meeting and went into Davis' office to talk things over.

"Davis I think I should handle the bulk of the home study. Your hatred for Jasmine practically flows from your pores. I think I can do a better job of keeping my cool in this situation. What do you think?"

"I hate to put you through this especially with you being pregnant and all but you're right, I can barely control myself." Davis admitted as he brushed his hand through his hair in frustration.

Trish walked behind Davis and began to massage his neck and shoulders planting a kiss on top his head.

"It'll all be o.k. I feel it in my soul. Just try to keep as positive as you can. I realize that's hard to do but I know you can do it. I love you." Trish hugged Davis and nibbled on his ear a little before turning his chair around and sitting in his lap.

"Kiss me." Trish ordered. Davis complied immediately while one of the babies kicked at him.

"Hey men, settle down in there can't you see your mother and I are busy right now?" He kissed her over and over and rubbed her belly gently, lovingly.

"That's better. See how well they listen, they're such good boys."

"Yes they are but I have to get going now, Melissa's due back today and I can't wait to see her. I really missed her." Trish kissed Davis one last time and left the office. For the first time she felt good about the outcome of the Jasmine situation.

When Trish and Duke walked through the doors of Celebrations Melissa squealed in delight. She looked wonderful! Rested, tanned, relaxed, and really happy. Melissa gave Trish and Duke each a hug as they walked into Trish's office. Melissa told them all about their trip and how much she loved the Hawaiian Islands. She thanked Trish over and over again as she rambled on and on. After the conversation began to wind down Trish got up the nerve to ask Melissa and Larry to dinner.

"I have some things we need to talk about, nothing bad, and I thought it would be better to do it outside the office so we won't be interrupted too much. Although between Zeus and Aimee I can't make any promises on that. Would tonight be alright?"

"Okay, let me check with Larry and I'll let you know in a few minutes." Melissa looked worried despite Trish's reassurances. Ten minutes later Melissa told Trish they could make it tonight.

"Great! About seven work for you?"

"Yeah. That's fine." Melissa answered warily. Melissa already knew about the triplets so what's wrong now?

After dinner the four of them went into Davis' office. Trish was nervous despite this being good news for everyone. Davis pulled out the contract Jake had drawn up and handed it to Larry to look over.

"Melissa I've decided, and Davis agrees, to give you forty percent of Celebrations, meaning instead of you being an employee you'd now be my partner. Do you think that's something you'd like to do?" Trish asked nervously.

"Duh! I'd love it but I don't think I could afford to buy forty percent of the company from you."

"No, no. This wouldn't cost you a cent, it's a gift. You know the company as well as I do and we work really well together. Frankly you've worked your ass off for me and you deserve it. You've earned it."   "Oh, and it would more than triple your income, I forgot that part."

Melissa looked over at Larry for confirmation as he finished looking over the contract.

"That's exactly what this contract says Melissa. It's up to you but as your attorney and boyfriend I recommend you sign it before they change their minds." Larry laughed as he grabbed a pen for Melissa to sign.

"I can't believe this is happening. Thank you so much, what can I say?"

"How about yes." Davis said.

"Yes!" Melissa shouted as she took the pen from Larry and signed on the dotted line.

"Now what?"

"Well first we have to hire some additional staff and get them trained before the holidays. I already put an ad in the paper and I've gotten a few responses that we need to look over and set-up some interviews. I have a feeling we need to hurry on this. I don't think you and I should need to attend the functions anymore. I was thinking you and I could do the presentations and planning and then let the others attend the events. They'll have a file containing all the information necessary for that event. We could have maybe a standardized form for each event to reduce human error. Sort of like a checklist or things to do list, something like that. What do you think?"

"I think you're a genius and you can invite me to dinner anytime you damn well please."

"I don't feel like talking business right now, let's leave that for tomorrow and celebrate tonight. All those in favor raise your hands." Trish laughed. Everyone, including Trish, raised their hands.

It was so much fun sitting and talking with Melissa and Larry. They talked about Hawaii and all things good and relaxing. Trish realized that this was the first time they had adult company that didn't involve a play date since they'd been married the first time.

When Trish entered the office the next day Melissa was at her desk and Sylvia was sitting in the reception area talking to Melissa.

"Hey there Sylvia how are you?" Trish asked as she kissed her cheek.

"Great. Actually I need to talk to both of you since the grapevine tells me you two are partners now. I want to apply for a job."

Trish was sure she wasn't hearing correctly.

"What? You want to work for us?" Melissa asked incredulously.

"Tell me what you're thinking Sylvia, I know you well enough to know you have a plan. Spill it." Trish said.

"Okay. I was thinking I could work two mornings a week and help with the planning aspect of the business. With my contacts and your good reputation I think I could bring in a lot of business with the society set. I would be sort of a liaison until I'm ready to fly on my own. What do you think?"

Trish and Melissa looked at each other and smiled. In unison they answered.

"When can you start?"

"Whenever you're ready, you tell me."

"We need to work out some space issues. Let's say in two weeks? Is that alright?" Trish asked.

"Works for me. See you two weeks from today at nine sharp."

"Wow. I never saw that one coming." Trish said as she plopped down into a chair.

"Same here, but I think it's brilliant really." Melissa added.

"We need to get our ducks in a row here, fast. What do you think about making the conference room into cubicles with those portable wall thingies. We could do our presentations in my office until we can build you your own office and another conference room."

"Sounds like a plan."

"I'll leave the shopping to you on all that and I'll work on creating the interoffice forms we can use. I'll also try and find an architect to get going on the construction plans."

Chapter 29

As Tom had predicted, Davis got a call from Child Services requesting a home study visit. They wanted to come out that day but Davis put them off for a couple more days and agreed to Friday at three o'clock when he knew Trish would be there. Just when he thought he had his anger suppressed it would come bubbling up from his toes and overtake him. Thank goodness he had Trish. Now that Aimee had started kindergarten she got home from school at four in the afternoon and that would give Davis and Trish some time alone with the Child Services worker. When Friday rolled around Davis was nervous as a cat but Trish handled everything beautifully. She conducted the tour of the house and introduced him to Josie, Duke, Zeus and Romeo. Davis was really glad they had taken the time for the obedience classes for Zeus, he behaved brilliantly. When they were seated in the living room Aimee came bursting in the door, excited to tell them about her fun day at school. She jumped onto Davis' lap as she leaned over to kiss Trish hello, raspberries first of course, and then Davis. She didn't realize someone else was even in the room until she turned around and saw him sitting in the wing backed chair.

"Hi. Who are you?"

"Aimee this is Mr. Woods and he's here to visit with us today." Trish said smoothly. Aimee accepted this information without question as she said to Mr. Woods.

"Look what I made in school today. This is my house and thewe's Zeus and Womeo and over hewrs mommy and daddy and Josie and Duke. Look I even put the free babies in mommy's tummy." She was so proud that she remembered all the details.

"Why did you put three babies in mommies tummy instead of just one?" Mr. Woods asked.

"Cause that's how many awe in thewe, isn't that wight daddy?"

"Yes it is baby. My wife's carrying triplets due in December." Davis said calmly.

"Wow! I can't imagine that. My wife just had one at a time and she could barely handle that."

"We've got Josie to help and we also made arrangements for her sister Helen to help too if necessary. I'm planning on staying home as long as possible with the babies, maybe even permanently if I feel too bad about leaving them. I'll have to wait and see how I feel about that when the time comes. I'm open on that and Davis is supportive on that issue as well. Aimee, I think Josie made you a special after school snack, why don't you go see what it is while the adults talk a little more." Trish suggested.

"Okay. Nice to meet you Mr. Woods." Aimee said politely.

When Aimee was out of ear shot Trish asked her questions.

"Mr. Woods will you be doing a home study like this for Jasmine as well?"

"Yes. I've actually had a few appointments with her already but she hasn't shown up for any of them yet, so we'll see what happens there."

"How will we know the result of our home study?" Trish asked.

"I can tell you right now actually. I find this home very suitable and Aimee seems happy and well adjusted. You have a very good support system in place even after you have the triplets and at this point I have no concerns about Aimee or the two of you. You need to also understand that I may have the same conclusions once I do Jasmine's home study so I don't want to give you any false hopes." He concluded.

"I appreciate your honesty and I just want to clarify that I hope you do find her home suitable. I think if it turns out that Jasmine is acceptable to be a mother to Aimee it can only benefit her to have another person who loves her. My main concern right now is how we did with ours." Trish said calmly.

"Well then I guess we're done here. Thank you for your time. I'll send a copy of my report to your attorney." Mr. Woods shook Davis' hand then Trish's and added.

"Good luck with the babies."

When Davis closed the door they both let out a sigh of relief.

"What was all that bullshit about hoping Jasmine's home study went well?"

"It's true that Aimee would benefit from a loving mother, unfortunately we all know that Jasmine is a scum sucking bottom feeder who couldn't mother a flea. I just left that last part out."

Trish jumped suddenly as one of the babies kicked her hard.

"You need to have a talk with the tribe in there, the natives are getting restless." Davis laughed and rubbed Trish's belly trying to make the ache go away.

"Tonight we'll have a pow wow." Davis promised.

As the weeks went by things at the office and at home began to take shape. Trish and Melissa rented additional office space next door to theirs and busted out the wall to make Melissa her office and add a conference room and the construction was almost done. They were down to trim work and carpet installation. Melissa had ordered the furniture for her office and it would be delivered as soon as the carpet was done. The cubicle's in the conference room were working out well. The employees they had hired seemed to be doing a good job and so was Sylvia. She was right, her name brought in quite a few clients and Sylvia was having a ball working with them.

At home the babies room was ready for furniture. Aimee had helped pick out the colors and quite a few toys as she considered herself the expert in the toy department. Trish loved the calming feel of the pale green walls of the nursery. She often found herself wandering into the room and sitting in the rocking chair, calmly rocking and letting her imagination wander to the time when the babies came home. She rubbed her belly and hummed a lullaby while she opened the drawers of the dressers to make sure everything was in place. They had practically filled the closet with diapers and Trish knew they would use each and every one. *Only two months to go.* Then her life would change all over again. Davis walked in just as Trish had begun to massage her head, she had been having headaches for the past couple of days and attributed it to stress. Davis took over the massage as he questioned her about the headaches.

"I've noticed you've been having some headaches recently, did you talk to Dr. McNeil about them?"

"No, I forgot all about it until just now when the headache came back."

"I'm calling him right now then. I need to know you and the boys are all right." Before Trish could turn around Davis was out the door.

A few minutes later Davis rushed back into the room.

"I just got off the phone with Dr. McNeil and he wants me to take you to the hospital. He said not to worry but he just wants to examine you to be sure. He'll meet us there and I already told Josie so let's get going." Davis said briskly.

"I hate to make him leave his family to meet us at the hospital, it's probably nothing."

"That's why he makes the big bucks. Let's go." Trish waddled behind Davis to the car.

At the hospital Dr. McNeil did a quick exam on Trish and told it like it was.

"I think you're in a pre-toxemia state. What that basically means is your blood pressure is slightly elevated and that in turn is dangerous to both you and the babies. I'd like to stay away from any medications for as long as possible and the best way to do that is complete bed rest and laying on your left side for the duration of the pregnancy. You can get up and use the bathroom and get up to come to your doctor's appointments and that's it. The rest of the time your down laying on your left side. To start out we'll let you do this at home, do you have someone who can come and look after her?"

"Yes, we have a live in nanny and housekeeper who can look after her." Davis answered as if Trish wasn't even in the room.

"Good. That will help a lot. I want to see you in my office in one week and we'll re-evaluate the situation then. The longer you can hold onto these babies the better off all of you will be. Watch your sodium intake as well and I'll see you next week. If you have any more headaches that won't go away with Tylenol I want you to call me immediately. Headaches are your bodies warning sign, listen to them. Take care."

"Davis you were absolutely right about this. I feel so stupid to not have realized something was wrong. I had no idea a headache was a warning sign. I promise I'll do everything the doctor says because now I'm scared." Trish said tearfully. Davis didn't say anything as he shot out of the room without a word. He came back a few minutes later stuffing a prescription into his shirt pocket.

"Where'd you go? Are you alright?"

"Yeah, I just had a question and I wanted to ask Dr. McNeil before he left."

"What was the question?"

"You seem to get upset lately a lot easier than you normally do so I asked if there was something we should do to help keep you calm. He gave me a prescription for a mild sedative that's safe during pregnancy."

"Is it for you to take or me?" Trish asked, honestly confused.

"Baby it's for you but only if you need it. Just make sure you let me know if you're upset about something. Don't try to be brave and hide it from me, it's not good for you or the boys. Promise me you'll tell me."

"You got it stud, now can we go home. I'm tired."

"I'll go get the car and bring it around to the doors. The nurse will come and get you to wheel you out." Davis kissed her and took off quickly.

On the drive home Trish started to list the phone calls she'd have to make.

"I already called Melissa and told her you're done working until after the babies are born. When I told her that she said she was calling Sylvia to see if she could give her more hours every week. Everything's under control so don't worry. If Melissa has any questions she can call you tomorrow, there's a phone right beside the bed for you. I called Josie and made sure she picked up some low sodium foods and let her know she'd be taking care of you from now on. She was really happy that she was going to have someone to talk to. Oh, and she asked me to ask you if you like scrabble. Apparently she loves it and plays it with Helen all the time. I told her you'd probably appreciate a few games every now and then, kind of breaks up the day. I also told her to have Duke move a television into our bedroom and have the cable company hook you up. If you'll give me a list of books you might like I'll pick them up for you tomorrow. How about puzzles, do you like puzzles?" Davis was rambling a hundred miles an hour as worry line creased his face.

Trish grabbed his hand and squeezed it gently.

"I love you. Don't worry about me I'll be fine. You know I'm very good at following doctor's orders and I promise you I'll do everything to the letter. I'll get upset if I think you're worrying about me so let's both do some deep breathing when we get home and relax. I think a good stiff drink will do you a world of good tonight. Maybe two even." Trish smiled at Davis and that relaxed him more than any drink would. She looked contented and relaxed, determined to do whatever necessary to keep herself and the babies healthy.

Everyone made the necessary adjustments to handle Trish's bed rest and they soon fell into a routine. Every day after Aimee had her snack she played Go Fish with Trish and kept her laughing with stories about what happened in school that day. Josie served dinner every night in Trish and Davis' bedroom on t.v. trays so they could still have dinner together. Aimee loved eating in the bedroom because she said it made her feel like a princess. Davis spent every night next to Trish in bed while he read or they watched television, usually ending in a cuddling session and a team meeting with *'the boys'*. Trish and Davis had begun thinking of names for the babies. Of course Davis refused to discuss any girls names. *What was the point-they were having boys.* One day Trish asked Davis

"Did you call Dr. McNeil to find out the sex of the babies? You know we agreed to be surprised and not find out ahead of time." Trish accused.

"No, I don't need to talk to Dr. McNeil about it because I know already, boys."

Davis said without a hint of hesitation. He almost had Trish convinced he really did know.

When it came to names everyone had an opinion and everyone knew someone named a name Trish liked who was a complete asshole. There were quite a few names that she and Davis agreed on, now all they had to do was narrow down the list to three.

Trish's doctor appointments had been going well. Everything was stable and Dr. McNeil was pleased that they didn't have to resort to any medications. Three weeks into her bed rest Trish and Davis were notified of a court date about Jasmine's petition for visitation with Aimee. Trish wouldn't be able to go but she made Davis promise to call her as soon as he walked out of the courtroom. Trish asked Davis to see if they could postpone any visitation until after the holidays if the court did end up ordering them.

 Trish tried not to watch the clock but the suspense was killing her. Josie stayed in the room with her to make sure she didn't have to give her a sedative. For a while it was touch and go as Trish did some deep breathing exercises. Finally the phone rang and Trish grabbed it quickly and answered.

"What happened?"

"It's all over baby. Jasmine was arrested for solicitation here in Harbor Springs and when they did their background check they found out about the warrant in New Mexico so she's in jail without bond and waiting to be transported back to New Mexico. Tom talked to the investigators in New Mexico and they feel they have a pretty tight case against her. On top of all that she never did keep any appointments with the Child Services worker and, get this, if she's convicted in New Mexico the judge said he would terminate Jasmine's parental rights. That means you could officially adopt Aimee. Tom also found a link between Jasmine and Sean and he turned over that information to both the FBI and the Harbor Springs police department. Whatever the evidence was Tom felt it proved that Jasmine was part of the whole kidnapping ordeal. She'll never bother us again baby. We're free." Davis was so relieved he was having trouble maintaining control as tears slid silently down his cheeks.

Trish heard Sylvia's voice in the background and was relieved that Davis wasn't alone.

"Can you come home?"

"On my way baby."

Chapter 30

One minute your lying in bed on your left side and the next you're on your way to the hospital in an ambulance. *Things can turn on a dime.* She had been laying down when all of the sudden she felt the gush of her water breaking. She called Dr. McNeil and he called the ambulance for her as Josie helped her change clothes and get ready to go to the hospital. Josie called Davis but he was in a deposition so the secretary refused to interrupt them. Trish called Jake and told him the situation and he took care of it for her. By the time Trish got to the hospital Dr. McNeil was standing at the emergency room door waiting for her. After a quick examination he ordered her prepped for a c-section. Trish had known she was going to have a c-section all along but she didn't want to go through it alone. Where was Davis?

Trish started to panic as she thought about giving birth without Davis there. Dr. McNeil ordered Trish sedated and told her if she didn't calm down he would have to knock her out so she tried some deep breathing until the sedative kicked in. The nurse was just finishing scrubbing Trish for surgery when Davis came rushing into the delivery room. Trish wanted to cry but held back so they didn't knock her out.

"Hey baby are you ready to say hello to the boys?" Davis asked.

"Now that you're here I am. I was so scared you wouldn't make it in time and Dr. McNeil threatened to knock me out if I didn't calm down." Trish had tears running down her face but she wasn't hysterical.

"I know I saw Dr. McNeil in the hallway and he told me about it. He wants to try to give us a few minutes to settle down before he starts. How are you feeling?"

"Numb from the waist down and ready to get this over with."

Dr. McNeil breezed through the door and looked at a calmed down Trish and started to deliver the babies. Behind him stood three nurses with towels draped over their hands, waiting for a baby to be put into their waiting arms.

Davis held Trish's hand as they waited for the first baby to be born. It didn't take long before Dr. McNeil said loudly.

"We have a boy here." He passed the baby to one of the nurses.

Trish was so happy she began to weep along with Davis. A few minutes later they heard another announcement.

"We have another boy here." The next nurse in line took that baby to tend to. Trish and Davis now heard some crying coming from each of their tiny precious babies.

"Well who wants to guess what sex the last baby is?" Dr. McNeil asked.

Davis said without hesitation.

"It's a boy."

Dr. McNeil looked up in disbelief.

"You're right. How'd you know?"

"Hey, I'm the dad. I know these things." Davis said in a cocky manner.

"Well if crying is any indication they sound very healthy. We'll have their weights for you in a second and let you hold them. Okay we have five pounds three ounces, five pounds six ounces, and finally five pounds four ounces. All very respectable weights, you did a good job holding onto these guys there mom, they're cooked just right."

The three nurses approached Trish and Davis and put two babies into Trish's arms and one into Davis' arms. They were absolutely the most beautiful babies Trish had ever seen. She cried with joy as one of the nurses wiped her tears for her. They all had a rather thick and unruly crop of dark hair and blue eyes. Trish and Davis counted their fingers and toes before they were taken back by the nurses to be examined and cleaned up. As Dr. McNeil finished suturing Trish he asked.

"So, what are their names?"

"Blaine, Kevin, and Trevor."

"Nice." Dr. McNeil said approvingly.

"Is anyone other than Josie in the waiting room?" Suddenly Trish was curious.

"Are you kidding, everyone's here. Once you tell Jake something it gets around quick. Good call going straight to him by the way."

"Maybe you should go tell everyone you were right."

"In a few minutes. I want to spend some more time with my bride." He bent down and kissed Trish lovingly on the lips.

"Thank you for my boys baby. They're as beautiful as their mother."

Once Trish and Davis were settled into their hospital room and the babies had been wheeled in the visitors descended en masse on the babies. Everyone was cooing and talking at the same time and the noise level increased even more as various hospital staff came in the see the triplets as the news spread throughout the hospital. Those dear boys slept through it all, as if this reaction was expected and tolerated. Trish let Aimee crawl into bed with her as Davis picked up one of the babies and placed him gently into Aimee's lap. Trish coached her about how to handle the baby. Aimee was so gentle and loving, almost too loving. She continually wanted to kiss each baby over and over. Davis let her kiss them but warned her they were too young for raspberries. As much as Trish loved everyone all she could think of was having some private time with Davis and the babies. She wanted to hold and cuddle them and get to know them without the constant interruption of guests. Davis must have felt the same way because Trish saw Davis pull Jake aside for a minute and then suddenly Jake was herding everyone out of the room, promising to come back tomorrow.

Trish and Davis took one baby at a time and examined them from head to toe and decided which one suited which name they had selected. They cuddled and cooed and stroked each baby, both together and individually, gently kissing each tiny hand and caressed each little cheek with their fingers. All of the babies seemed to have a strong grip as they grabbed the offered finger and held on tight. Feeding time was hectic at first but luckily Davis had experience in this department and Trish gladly accepted any advice he gave. By the time they were done feeding all the babies Trish and Davis were exhausted. When the nurses aid delivered Trish and Davis' dinner she found them both sound asleep on Trish's bed holding each other in their arms. She set the trays down but didn't have the heart to wake them. She tip-toed out of the room. Trish woke two hours later when one of the babies had started to fuss a little. She quietly slipped out of bed and changed Kevin's diaper then picked up her little miracle and took him to the rocking chair. Trish sat holding him, talking in a whisper to him as she fed him smoothly, as if she had been doing this all her life. She told him how much she loved him and would take care of him. Davis laid on the bed, awake, as he watched Trish bond with their his son. He was now the father of three boys and a girl he realized and his heart felt a twinge of fear.

He recalled Aimee's birth and couldn't help but compare the two experiences, realizing they were exact opposites. What a difference it made when you were in love with the mother of your baby. It made the whole experience wondrous and joyous instead of tense and hostile. These boys were lucky to have a mother like Trish and he was going to make sure they knew it because Davis knew now that motherhood was not instinctual, but followed the heart of the mother, and their mother's heart was made of gold. Davis knew it wasn't going to be easy raising three boys and a girl but one thing was for sure, it would never be boring. Davis got out of bed when Blaine and Trevor started fussing and went over and changed Trevor's diaper, then Blaine's next. While Davis did diaper duty Trish exchanged a sleeping Kevin with a very hungry Trevor. She went back to the rocking chair and fed Trevor, talking and caressing him, telling him how much she loved him. Davis grabbed a bottle, sat across from Trish and fed Blaine. He nuzzled the little boys neck and kissed his wild mass of hair. All the boys hair stuck straight up on the top of their heads. No amount of combing could tame the wild hair and for some reason Davis took that as a good sign.

"Wow. That went a lot smoother than the first time we fed them. I think we're already getting the hang of this triplet thing." Davis said with amazement.

"Yeah, I think we make a pretty good team here daddy-o." Trish laughed.

Both Blaine and Trevor were sound asleep but neither one of them wanted to get up and put them back into their bassinette's. Davis got up and put Blaine into Trish's other arm and went and got the sleeping Kevin. He sat back down to rock him as he also slept contentedly. Trish and Davis stared down at the babies, completely absorbed in the little faces they made as they slept. Trish and Davis laughed softly and were completely absorbed as they watched their boys, the five of them bonding silently as their hearts conversed.

After two months of caring for the babies Davis and Trish realized that the house they now occupied was going to be too small to raise this family in. They discussed just adding on but decided they needed a bigger yard for the kids and the dog, who was now the size of a small pony. Zeus was a gentle giant who loved everyone. He intimidated with his sheer massive size so strangers didn't want to get near him as he stood at the fence watching the world go by.

Trish and Davis started house hunting with a vengeance. They didn't want a house so big that they would never see each other, they believed in family togetherness yet they realized they would need at least five bedrooms as the boys got older. After three months and what seemed like hundreds of homes they decided on a recently refurbished farm house with four bedrooms and twenty acres, twelve of these acres were still heavily wooded, which would be perfect for young boys to explore. Trish and Davis decided to add on a master suite for themselves, including their own bathroom and an attached apartment for Josie. They let Aimee take what was now the biggest bedroom, after all she had seniority and more possessions than anyone else in the house. The boys were all staying in the same room for now and one of the bedrooms was turned into a playroom. Trish loved the open feeling of the house and the loft on the second floor allowed you to look down into the family room and kitchen at the same time. The front of the house had a formal living room, dining room and library/office combination, which were fine for entertaining, but they all preferred the informal back of the house. One entire wall in the family room was all glass and French doors that looked out into the backyard and the woods beyond. There was a large patio immediately outside the French doors and near the kitchen, Trish loved the little pass-through window in the kitchen leading to the patio. Someone put a lot of thought into the construction of the house and Trish didn't want to disturb the country charm of it with the additions they planned. She didn't want their suite and the apartment to feel like additions but part of the original structure. They continued with the hardwood floors in all the additions and even paid extra, believe it or not, for the distressed look of the wood to match the rest of the wood floors in the house. Doorways were arched instead of square and antique furniture was used to furnish the suite.

As all this construction went on and the torture of moving and caring for three infants took over Trish's days she realized more and more that she wanted to stay home with the boys full time. Davis wanted her to be happy, so he would support any decision she made. Trish realized how blessed she was to be in a position to even have a choice of whether to stay home or not. Now a days stay at home mom's were generally looked down upon by working women but Trish didn't care, this was the decision that was right for her and her family. Trish thought about the women who had to work no matter what and that led her to thinking about how she could help them. She also wanted to help women who wanted to work but stayed home because they were fearful of picking a bad day care situation, especially if the child was too young to talk. Suddenly she found herself formulating a daycare concept unlike any other she had ever heard about, and she thought it was a good one. She decided to talk to Davis, halfway hoping he would talk her out of it.

"Davis I have an idea I want to talk to you about, do you think we could have some time alone together after dinner tonight?" Trish asked over the phone as she talked to him for his mid-day baby update.

"Uh, oh. What's wrong?"

"Nothing bad, really. Just an idea about a business venture I had."

"Okay, do you want me to come home early tonight?" Davis offered.

"That would be great! I actually had two ideas really, and one is pure hot monkey sex. It's the other idea that's business."

"Oh, really. What are you wearing right now?"

"Absolutely nothing but a smile."

"Just lying in bed and waiting for my man to get home."

If he only knew she was in sweat pants and a t-shirt with baby puke on it and hadn't had a chance to take a shower yet. Another miracle had been that she had slowly gotten her figure back after the babies. Trish had thought she'd been thoroughly horrified when she was pregnant, but the first time she saw her image in a mirror after the birth of the boys had her bursting into tears instantly, sure she'd never be herself again. It was a long time before she would let Davis see her naked.

Chapter 31

Once Trish and Davis were done with their hot monkey sex, which had been really, really hot, they moved onto the business aspect of their meeting. Trish chuckled as she thought that at least they still had their priority's straight by having the sex first.

"What are you laughing at?" Davis asked as he lay naked in bed with the woman he loved, naked also, wrapped in his arms.

"I love our priority system, sex first, business later. It's perfect." Trish said as she kissed him passionately.

"I'll talk business now to give you a few minutes to recover. My idea is to start a private child care business in the same office building, hopefully even on the same floor as Celebrations and the law firm."

"I thought you decided to stay home with the kids for a while."

"I did and I am, I was thinking of someone else to run it, maybe Josie's sister Helen. Josie says that since her husband died and her kids are out of the house she's so lonely and I want someone who's raised a family to run it, not someone who took it in college. Helen's still young enough to have the energy for running a business and of course I could send Josie to help out in a pinch. I want this to be private at first, only for employees of the law firm and Celebrations, if Helen chooses to expand at a later date that's up to her. What do you think? Stupid idea, right?"

"I'm not sure, tell me your motivation for this and what you hope to accomplish with it."

"That's the really cool part. I realized how blessed I am to have the choice of whether or not I want to stay home with the kids. Most women don't have that choice, they have to work and so do the men. With this child care each parent would have a video and audio feed throughout the day to check on their kids and if they choose to, they can come and have lunch and breaks with their kids. They'd have total access and the convenience of having their children right down the hall instead of wildly driving around town in a hurry to pick-up their kids and frazzled to the bone by the time they get home. They would know what their children ate, when or if they took a nap, how they interact with other children. If their child is an infant they'll be able to see someone holding their baby and feeding them in a rocking chair, not someone propping-up a bottle with a rolled up blanket and walking away. My goal is not to educate but to nurture happy little human beings. If they accidentally get a little education at the same time through play then all the better. In the beginning I'd like to start out with the age group of zero to five years old. Once children are in school there are latchkey programs that would be easier and a lot less expensive than our program. Well, now tell me it's a stupid idea."

"I can't tell you that. I think it's brilliant and heartfelt, just like you. It would never occur to most women to think of people other than themselves after giving birth to triplets, yet you have compassion and empathy for them. I love you even more than I thought was ever possible. I think you should go for it, talk to Jake about it. Sylvia may be a good choice as an administrator."

"Okay, I'll talk to Jake. I might even persuade him to pick-up part of the tab and make it a benefit to his employees. I love you too, have you recovered yet?" She asked while she began to kiss, lick, and nibble her way down Davis' body. Davis tried to answer but all he could get out were moans and sighs of pleasure as Trish took over his body and mind with her mouth. At times like this both Trish and Davis were glad they'd had their suite soundproofed.

Trish talked to Jake about the child care center and he thought it was an excellent idea. He even agreed to pick-up half the child care expenses for his employees. Helen agreed to handle the child care aspect and Sylvia took over the administrative duties. Trish wished it had been a smooth start but Sylvia and Helen often butted heads in the beginning, putting Trish in the middle as the mediator. For Trish it was hard to step back and watch other people put her dream into action, but she knew she wanted to be with her kids more than anything.

The boys were growing so fast Trish didn't know where the time went. At fourteen months they were all walking now and getting into everything! Aimee loved to play chase with the boys and they squealed in delight as she chased them around the yard along with Zeus barking loudly. Davis allowed the boys to tackle him and roughhoused with them. They giggled when he tickled them, they were all boy, including Davis. Trish and

Aimee usually looked on as their nail polish dried. Mostly they looked at each other and shrugged their shoulder in a *'why do they* do that' gesture, then went back to their nails. It was very important to Trish that Aimee felt like she belonged with them and was part of the family. Aimee knew Trish wasn't her real mother, and often wished she was, but she was secure in the knowledge that no biological mother could love her more than Trish did.

One day Trish and Davis called Aimee into the library to talk to her. She was sure she was in trouble and she walked like she was being led to the gallows. When she sat down she blurted out "I didn't do anything wrong!" Almost bursting into tears.
"I know sweetheart, we didn't call you in here because you're in trouble. Just the opposite, really." Davis reassured.
"I'm sorry if you thought you were in trouble baby. We didn't mean to scare you." Trish added.
"We just need to talk to you for a few minutes. Today I got a call from a detective in New Mexico, where your biological mother lived, and he told me that she had an accident and that, well she went to heaven. Do you understand what that means?" Davis asked.
"That means she doesn't live on earth anymore."
"Right. How do you feel about that? It means that you'll never get to meet her. Does that upset you or make you sad?" Trish questioned.
Aimee sat and thought for a few minutes then looked Trish straight in the eyes and answered.
"You're my mother. I never met her so I never missed her so, no, it doesn't bother me. I feel bad that she's not on earth anymore but I'm not sad."
"One other thing this means, and I want you to think about this before you answer, is that now Trish can legally adopt you. That would make Trish officially and legally your mommy no matter what. Do you think that's something you would like to do?" Davis asked. He expected some hesitation on Aimee's part but was stunned as she leapt out of the chair and straight into Trish's arms.
"I want you to be my mommy forever and ever."

Trish hugged Aimee tightly and kissed her head.

"Aimee nothing would make me happier or more proud than to be your mommy forever and ever. Daddy, could you do the paperwork for us?" Trish asked.

"Absolutely! I'm so happy and proud of you both. I'm the luckiest daddy in the world."

After Aimee skipped out of the room Trish burst into tears.

"I've wanted this for so long. I'm so happy." Davis hugged her and let her cry it out as he rubbed her back and kissed her hair.

Things for the Sinclair family had begun to run like a finely tuned machine. Everyone had their jobs to do in both the mornings and evenings, which kept everything running smoothly. If someone didn't do their job the rest of them fell like dominoes and the guilty party heard about it from everyone else.

Trish stopped in as often as possible to Celebrations and the child care center. Both businesses were thriving and Melissa had never been happier, making sure she let Trish know every chance she got.

When Trish felt she had interrupted everyone's day enough at Celebrations, she moved on to join Davis in his office.

■ ■

"Hey baby, what a nice surprise! I didn't know you were coming to town today." He stood to kiss her hello.

"Yeah, well, I think it's important to keep you guessing. Keeps you on your toes."

"Are you busy for the next half hour or so? If you are it's okay, I just thought." "What'd you have in mind?" He wiggled his eyebrows."Not that! I have an appointment with Dr. McNeil and I thought you could come along." "Sure. I haven't seen him in a while. Are you afraid something's wrong?"

■ ■

"No, nothing's wrong." But she didn't say it very convincingly.

Davis held her hand as they rode up in the elevator to Dr. McNeil's office. They were shown into an examination room and Trish did a little striptease for Davis while getting ready for her examination.

Dr. McNeil came bounding into the room.

"Well if it isn't the Sinclair's, my favorite patients. How are you Davis?" He shook Davis' hand.

"Great!"

"How are my favorite triplets?"

"All happy and healthy." Trish replied.

"Good. Glad to hear it." Dr. McNeil looked over Trish's chart before beginning the examination. He shot Trish a look of surprise but didn't say anything.

"Let's see what we have here." He proceeded with the exam, making small talk the whole time. When he was finished he helped Trish sit up.

"I'll see you in my office, the nurse will show you the way after you're done dressing." And he whisked out of the room.

Davis had an incredible feeling of déjà vu as he sat there holding Trish's hand, only this time he wasn't nervous at all.

Dr. McNeil burst through the door and took a seat behind his desk. He looked up and said simply.

"Congratulations, again." Dr. McNeil laughed.

Davis looked at Trish, who was smiling broadly.

"Hot Damn!" Davis clapped his hands loudly.

"Just don't think this time it's a boy, it better be a girl!" Trish laughed.

"Considering your medical history, I think we should take a quick peek and see what's what." Dr. McNeil advised.

"I'll have the nurse come and set you up in the ultrasound room."

"How do you really feel about this? Are you mad, glad, sad, what?"

"Thrilled. Excited. Incredulous. How about you?" Davis questioned.

"Thrilled. Excited. Nervous. Elated. All of the above." Trish answered.

When Dr. McNeil finished the ultrasound he looked at both of them with a huge smile on his face.

"Well. Spit it out." Davis demanded.

"I don't know the sex yet, it's too early to tell, but there are again three fetuses' in there. The chances of this happening twice without fertility drugs are astounding, one in a kazillion. Trish you're a medical marvel."

"Hey, don't forget me. I had a little something to do with it too you know." Davis said proudly.

173

Trish realized this was her life as it was meant to be. All the ups and downs and ins and outs. It was never meant to be a smooth ride or easy. She wouldn't trade it for anything in the world. *Thank God.*

She squeezed Davis' hand and counted her blessings, not in dollars and cents, or possessions, but in loving hearts.

Turn the page for the first chapter of Book Two of the Celebrations Trilogy.
CELEBRATION OF LOVE

CELEBRATION OF LIFE

Melissa sat in her office at Celebrations thinking about her baby brother, Jason, and the news he had just delivered. How could her baby brother be thinking of getting married? He's only twenty six, still a baby and wet behind the ears for cripes sake! Besides, she was the oldest so she was supposed to get married first. She wondered if her future sister in-law was pregnant, she had forgotten to ask Jason, she had been so shocked by the news. They barely knew each other and now they were jumping into marriage, they'd only been dating for a year. Melissa and Larry had been dating for two years themselves and never discussed marriage. Ever. Now she wondered why. She knew they both eventually wanted to get married and have children. Both of them were secure in their careers and made excellent money. Larry was a lawyer with the Sullivan Law Firm and had been for three years, and, as far as she knew, Jake Sullivan was happy with Larry's job performance. It also worked out well that Larry was Davis Sinclair's best friend, who just happened to be married to Melissa's best friend, Trish. Trish had given Melissa forty percent of Celebrations and made her president of the company when she was pregnant with her and Davis' triplet boys. Not that Melissa hadn't earned it, she had worked her ass off for seven years and was more than qualified to run the company for Trish. In the two years since Melissa had taken over running the company it had grown tremendously and she took pride in that fact. It didn't hurt that she was making more money than she have ever dreamed possible, allowing her to live a very comfortable life and still put money aside for retirement.

So why did she feel like there was a huge hole in her life. Something was missing. Melissa understood that life wasn't always fun and exciting, but was it supposed to be so ...boring? Was that what she was feeling, bored? At first it was easy to blame other things and people but in the end she was responsible for her own happiness. If she could just put her finger on what was missing. She wanted to feel completely fulfilled but wasn't sure that was possible. Was anyone ever completely happy? Trish was but that was because she had the guts to go after what she wanted. Was she jealous of Trish? Damn right she was.

Suddenly she wondered if Larry was happy. That was something they never discussed, were they happy with each other? Did they even love each other? Suddenly it felt like Melissa and Larry were together because it was just easier for both of them. They always knew they had a date for all their social occasions. A standing date every Friday night for dinner at Larry's, always take-out, and a movie. Good ol' Larry was steady and solid, a crutch that Melissa maybe took for granted. Sex with Larry was good, nothing to put into a romance novel or anything, but satisfying for both of them. Well that sounded nice and boring, as if it was just a bodily function necessary to perform every once in a while for normal existence and stress management. Wow, talk about being in a funk. She realized she wasn't exactly a ball of fire in the bedroom either. If Melissa wanted more fire and passion in her love life she needed to do something about it and quit whining. Tonight was their standing Friday night date, but it wasn't going to be boring any more.

Armed with a purpose she quickly tidied up her desk and grabbed her purse as she fled out of her office. A trip to Victoria's Secret was on the top of her to do list, along with a trip to the beauty salon for a complete make-over. She intended to be ready, willing and able by the time Larry got home tonight.

When Melissa walked into the lingerie store she couldn't believe the huge selection and quickly got overwhelmed. A salesperson approached immediately asking if she could help Melissa with something.

"May I help you find something?" The sales lady asked politely.

"Yes, please. I'm looking for something to make my boyfriend's eyes pop out of his head and another part of his anatomy to salute, if you get my meaning. Do you have anything like that?" Melissa laughed as she blushed to a crimson color.

"Absolutely, tell me what he likes." Well the saleslady had her there, she had no idea what Larry's idea of sexy was.

"I'm not sure really, I've never bought stuff like this for myself, or him, and I don't even know where to start." Melissa admitted sheepishly.

"Okay. Let's start with this, what's his favorite color?"

"Ummm, I think he'd like something in red or black, something that looks, I don't know, naughty or something that's against the rules. Does that make any sense to you?" Melissa asked.

"Yep. Let's go to the back of the store and I'll show you some things. You can try them on back there too."

I'm so nervous, isn't that just stupid? I am an adult and so is he so I'm just being silly.

When they got to the back of the store Melissa couldn't believe the large selection they had. She tried on a few things first in the pastel shades but didn't want anything that could be construed as bridal or virginal, she wanted hot. In the end she ended-up with a whole new wardrobe of matching bras and thongs for everyday and then the racier stuff she thought Larry would like. She even invested in some edible underwear. Tonight she would wear a black lace and satin demi-bra with matching thong, garter belt, and fish net stockings with a pair of fuck me shoes.

At the beauty salon she decided to have her already dark blonde hair highlighted and got a manicure and pedicure, choosing a hot red polish color for both toes and fingers. She loved the highlights and had allowed the stylist to cut her already shoulder length hair a little shorter and into a swingy, fun bob that looked like it would be easy to care for. It made her feel sassy and gave her confidence. It looked a lot better than her old fashioned, poker straight, boring hair style. Now her hair had bounce and shine and felt incredibly silky, she couldn't stop running her fingers through it. She hoped Larry would feel the same way.

Now all she needed to do was pick up their take-out dinner. One thing about Melissa was she could out eat most men and still keep her slim, athletic build. She supposed it helped that at five feet seven inches she could carry a little more weight than shorter women but she also jogged as often as possible in the park. She wished she had a more curvy figure but at least she had decent breasts, nothing huge mind you but enough, she thought, for a man to hold onto. Her worst feature were her feet, they were big. Larry often teased her about leaving her big foot prints in his snow, claiming people looking for a Yeti had come pounding on his door when they saw her tracks in the snow. At least she was graceful even with the big feet. Everything on Melissa's body existed on a perfectly straight vertical plain with her full mouth and warm brown eyes acting as punctuation marks for her open, friendly manner.

Melissa decided on Chinese food for dinner and as a last minute impulse, bought a large package of tea lights with holders to place around the family room to set the mood. She rented Fatal Attraction at the video store and raced to Larry's house. Melissa hoped they were going to be busy long before the bunny was boiled, she hated that part of the movie, being the animal lover that she was. Melissa let herself into Larry's house with her key and made several trips back and forth to the car, hauling in bag after bag.

Larry's idea of decorating was still early bachelor pad and he had no intention of upgrading or buying anything matching. The dark burgundy sofa was well worn velvet -like fabric with the seat cushions worn shiny in some spots. Two recliners flanked each side of the sofa, one was stained tan micro fiber and torn in several places which were taped with silver duct tape. The other chair was in better shape and powder blue but not very comfortable. He had a rectangle wooden coffee table that sat in front of the couch and had at one time been light oak. Now the only stain left was on the legs because the top was so worn the stain had been rubbed off. A huge big screen television was mounted on the wall opposite the couch and two mismatched lamps sat on end tables that once had matched the coffee table. Permanent bottle rings stained both coffee tables. The one thing Larry splurged on was a regular cleaning person because he was, for all intents and purposes, a neat person. Cheap, but neat.

The kitchen could be summed up in one word, white. Everything was white with the exception of the old gold refrigerator and the avocado green stove that Melissa refused to use. It was so old the last time she tried to use it the oven door handle came off in her hand. Melissa declared it a death trap and stayed away from it since then. Thank God for microwaves. He didn't have a kitchen table or dining room, he didn't need them because he always ate in front of the television in the family room. The living room and bedroom on the first floor were completely empty just like the two unused bedrooms upstairs. Larry's bedroom had a full sized mattress and box spring that sat on the floor and one large high boy dresser. That too had seen better days and had been his since childhood. Melissa thought if she ever lost her job at Celebrations she'd take up cleaning houses because whoever did Larry's had it easy.

Melissa hummed as she set out the candles and arranged their dinner plates. She had them ready to pop into the microwave whenever they were ready to eat. She decided to take a quick shower before she put on her lingerie and readied herself for what she expected to be a night of wild, passionate sex. She shivered with anticipation as she stepped out of the shower and slathered herself with the new body lotion and perfume she had bought at the beauty salon. Now all she had to do was wait for her man to come home. She sat on the couch and waited for Larry.

Visit my website at: http://patriciagauthier.com

www.ingramcontent.com/pod-product-compliance
Lightning Source LLC
Chambersburg PA
CBHW070919130626
46555CB00001B/203